The Wolf Hunters

James Oliver Curwood

Contents

CHAPTER I THE FIGHT IN THE FOREST 7
CHAPTER II HOW WABIGOON BECAME A WHITE MAN 15
CHAPTER III RODERICK SEES THE FOOTPRINT 21
CHAPTER IV RODERICK'S FIRST TASTE OF THE HUNTER'S LIFE 29
CHAPTER V MYSTERIOUS SHOTS IN THE WILDERNESS 39
CHAPTER VI MUKOKI DISTURBS THE ANCIENT SKELETONS 46
CHAPTER VII RODERICK DISCOVERS THE BUCKSKIN BAG 59
CHAPTER VIII HOW WOLF BECAME THE COMPANION OF MEN 67
CHAPTER IX WOLF TAKES VENGEANCE UPON HIS PEOPLE 77
CHAPTER X RODERICK EXPLORES THE CHASM 85
CHAPTER XI RODERICK'S DREAM 93
CHAPTER XII THE SECRET OF THE SKELETON'S HAND 99
CHAPTER XIII SNOWED IN 107
CHAPTER XIV THE RESCUE OF WABIGOON 118
CHAPTER XV RODERICK HOLDS THE WOONGAS AT BAY 127
CHAPTER XVI THE SURPRISE AT THE POST 134

THE WOLF HUNTERS

BY

James Oliver Curwood

To my comrades of the great northern wilderness, those faithful companions with whom I have shared the joys and hardships of the "long silent trail," and especially to Mukoki, my red guide and beloved friend, does the writer gratefully dedicate this volume

CHAPTER I
THE FIGHT IN THE FOREST

Cold winter lay deep in the Canadian wilderness. Over it the moon was rising, like a red pulsating ball, lighting up the vast white silence of the night in a shimmering glow. Not a sound broke the stillness of the desolation. It was too late for the life of day, too early for the nocturnal roamings and voices of the creatures of the night. Like the basin of a great amphitheater the frozen lake lay revealed in the light of the moon and a billion stars. Beyond it rose the spruce forest, black and forbidding. Along its nearer edges stood hushed walls of tamarack, bowed in the smothering clutch of snow and ice, shut in by impenetrable gloom.

A huge white owl flitted out of this rim of blackness, then back again, and its first quavering hoot came softly, as though the mystic hour of silence had not yet passed for the night-folk. The snow of the day had ceased, hardly a breath of air stirred the ice-coated twigs of the trees. Yet it was bitter cold--so cold that a man, remaining motionless, would have frozen to death within an hour.

Suddenly there was a break in the silence, a weird, thrilling sound, like a great sigh, but not human--a sound to make one's blood run faster and fingers twitch on rifle-stock. It came from the gloom of the tamaracks. After it there fell a deeper silence than before, and the owl, like a noiseless snowflake, drifted out over the frozen lake. After a few moments it came again, more faintly than before. One versed in woodcraft would have slunk deeper into the rim of blackness, and listened, and wondered, and watched; for in the sound he would have recognized the wild, half-conquered note of a wounded beast's suffering and agony.

Slowly, with all the caution born of that day's experience, a huge bull moose walked out into the glow of the moon. His magnificent head, drooping under the weight of massive antlers, was turned inquisitively across the lake to the north. His nostrils were distended, his eyes glaring, and he left behind a trail of blood. Half a mile away he caught the edge of the spruce forest. There something told him he would find safety. A hunter would have known that he was wounded unto death as he dragged himself out into the foot-deep snow of the lake.

A dozen rods out from the tamaracks he stopped, head thrown high, long ears pitched forward, and nostrils held half to the sky. It is in this attitude that a moose listens when he hears a trout splash three-quarters of a mile away. Now there was only the vast, unending silence, broken only by the mournful hoot of the snow owl on the other side of the lake. Still the great beast stood immovable, a little pool of blood growing upon the snow under his forward legs. What was the mystery that lurked in the blackness of yonder forest? Was it danger? The keenest of human hearing would have detected nothing. Yet to those long slender ears of the bull moose, slanting beyond the heavy plates of his horns, there came a sound. The animal lifted his head still higher to the sky, sniffed to the east, to the west, and back to the shadows of the tamaracks. But it was the north that held him.

From beyond that barrier of spruce there soon came a sound that man might have heard--neither the beginning nor the end of a wail, but something like it. Minute by minute it came more clearly, now growing in volume, now almost dying away, but every instant approaching--the distant hunting call of the wolf-pack! What the hangman's noose is to the murderer, what the leveled rifles are to the condemned spy, that hunt-cry of the wolves is to the wounded animal of the forests.

Instinct taught this to the old bull. His head dropped, his huge antlers leveled themselves with his shoulders, and he set off at a slow trot toward the east. He was taking chances in thus crossing the open, but to him the spruce forest was home, and there he might find refuge. In his brute brain he reasoned that he could get there before the wolves broke cover. And then--

Again he stopped, so suddenly that his forward legs doubled under him and he pitched into the snow. This time, from the direction of the wolf-pack, there came the ringing report of a rifle! It might have been a mile or two miles away, but distance did not lessen the fear it brought to the dying king of the North. That day he had heard the same sound, and it had brought mysterious and weakening pain in his vitals. With a supreme effort he brought himself to his feet, once more sniffed into the north, the east, and the west, then turned and buried himself in the black and frozen wilderness of tamarack.

Stillness fell again with the sound of the rifle-shot. It might have lasted five minutes or ten, when a long, solitary howl floated from across the lake. It ended in the sharp, quick yelp of a wolf on the trail, and an instant later was taken up by others, until the pack was once more in full cry. Almost simultaneously a figure darted out upon the ice from the edge of the forest. A dozen paces and it paused and turned back toward the black wall of spruce.

"Are you coming, Wabi?"

A voice answered from the woods. "Yes. Hurry up--run!"

Thus urged, the other turned his face once more across the lake. He was a youth of not more than eighteen. In his right hand he carried a club. His left arm, as if badly injured, was done up in a sling improvised from a lumberman's heavy scarf. His face was scratched and bleeding, and his whole appearance showed that he was nearing complete exhaustion. For a few moments he ran through the snow, then halted to a staggering walk. His breath came in painful gasps. The club slipped from his nerveless fingers, and conscious of the deathly weakness that was overcoming him he did not attempt to regain it. Foot by foot he struggled on, until suddenly his knees gave way under him and he sank down into the snow.

From the edge of the spruce forest a young Indian now ran out upon the surface of the lake. His breath was coming quickly, but with excitement rather than fatigue. Behind him, less than half a mile away, he could hear the rapidly approaching cry of the hunt-pack, and for an instant he bent his lithe form close to the snow, measuring with the acuteness of his race the distance of the pursuers. Then he looked for his white companion, and failed to see the motionless blot that marked where the other had fallen. A look of alarm shot into his eyes, and resting his rifle between his knees he placed his hands, trumpet fashion, to his mouth and gave a signal call which, on a still night like this, carried for a mile.

"Wa-hoo-o-o-o-o-o! Wa-hoo-o-o-o-o-o!"

At that cry the exhausted boy in the snow staggered to his feet, and with an answering shout which came but faintly to the ears of the Indian, resumed his flight across the lake. Two or three minutes later Wabi came up beside him.

"Can you make it, Rod?" he cried.

The other made an effort to answer, but his reply was hardly more than a gasp. Before Wabi could reach out to support him he had lost his little remaining strength and fallen for a second time into the snow.

"I'm afraid--I--can't do it--Wabi," he whispered. "I'm--bushed--"

The young Indian dropped his rifle and knelt beside the wounded boy, supporting his head against his own heaving shoulders.

"It's only a little farther, Rod," he urged. "We can make it, and take to a tree. We ought to have taken to a tree back there, but I didn't know that you were so far gone; and there was a good chance to make camp, with three cartridges left for the open lake."

"Only three!"

"That's all, but I ought to make two of them count in this light. Here, take hold of my shoulders! Quick!"

He doubled himself like a jack-knife in front of his half-prostrate companion. From behind them there came a sudden chorus of the wolves, louder and clearer than before.

"They've hit the open and we'll have them on the lake inside of two minutes," he cried. "Give me your arms, Rod! There! Can you hold the gun?"

He straightened himself, staggering under the other's weight, and set off on a half-trot for the distant tamaracks. Every muscle in his powerful young body was strained to its utmost tension. Even more fully than his helpless burden did he realize the peril at their backs.

Three minutes, four minutes more, and then--

A terrible picture burned in Wabi's brain, a picture he had carried from boyhood of another child, torn and mangled before his very eyes by these outlaws of the North, and he shuddered. Unless he sped those three remaining bullets true, unless that rim of tamaracks was reached in time, he knew what their fate would be. There flashed into his mind one last resource. He might drop his wounded companion and find safety for himself. But it was a thought that made Wabi smile grimly. This was not the first time that these two had risked their lives together, and that very day Roderick had fought valiantly for the other, and had been the one to suffer. If they died, it would be in company. Wabi made up his mind to that and clutched the other's arms in a firmer grip. He was pretty certain that death faced them both. They might escape the wolves, but the refuge of a tree, with the voracious pack on guard below, meant only a more painless end by cold. Still, while there was life there was hope, and he hurried on through the snow, listening for the wolves behind him and with each moment feeling more keenly that his own powers of endurance were rapidly reaching an end.

For some reason that Wabi could not explain the hunt-pack had ceased to give tongue. Not only the allotted two minutes, but five of them, passed without the appearance of the animals on the lake. Was it possible that they! had lost the trail? Then it occurred to the Indian that perhaps he had wounded one of the pursuers, and that the others, discovering his injury, had set upon him and were now participating in one of the cannibalistic feasts that had saved them thus far. Hardly had he thought of this possibility when he was thrilled by a series of long howls, and looking back he discerned a dozen or more dark objects moving swiftly over their trail.

Not an eighth of a mile ahead was the tamarack forest. Surely Rod could travel that distance!

"Run for it, Rod!" he cried. "You're rested now. I'll stay here and stop 'em!"

He loosened the other's arms, and as he did so his rifle fell from the white boy's nerveless grip and buried itself in the snow. As he relieved himself of his burden he saw for the first time the deathly pallor and partly closed eyes of his companion. With a new terror filling his own faithful heart he knelt beside the form which lay so limp and lifeless, his blazing eyes traveling from the ghastly face to the oncoming wolves, his rifle ready in his hands. He could now discern the wolves trailing out from the spruce forest like ants. A dozen of them were almost within rifle-shot. Wabi knew that it was with this vanguard of the pack that he must deal if he succeeded in stopping the scores behind. Nearer and nearer he allowed them to come, until the first were scarce two hundred feet away. Then, with a sudden shout, the Indian leaped to his feet and dashed fearlessly toward them. This unexpected move, as he had intended, stopped the foremost wolves in a huddled group for an instant, and in this opportune moment Wabi leveled his gun and fired. A long howl of pain testified to the effect of the shot. Hardly had it begun when Wabi fired again, this time with such deadly precision that one of the wolves, springing high into the air, tumbled back lifeless among the pack without so much as making a sound.

Running to the prostrate Roderick, Wabi drew him quickly upon his back, clutched his rifle in the grip of his arm, and started again for the tamaracks. Only once did he look back, and then he saw the wolves gathering in a snarling, fighting crowd about their slaughtered comrades. Not until he had reached the shelter of the tamaracks did the Indian youth lay down his burden, and then in his own exhaustion he fell prone upon the snow, his black eyes fixed cautiously upon the feasting pack. A few minutes later he discerned dark spots appearing here and there upon the whiteness of the snow, and at these signs of the termination of the feast he climbed up into the low branches of a spruce and drew Roderick after him. Not until then did the wounded boy show visible signs of life. Slowly he recovered from the faintness which had overpowered him, and after a little, with some assistance from Wabi, was able to place himself safely on a higher limb.

"That's the second time, Wabi," he said, reaching a hand down affectionately to the other's shoulder. "Once from drowning, once from the wolves. I've got a lot to even up with you!"

"Not after what happened to-day!"

The Indian's dusky face was raised until the two were looking into each other's eyes, with a gaze of love, and trust. Only a moment thus, and instinctively their glance turned toward the lake. The wolf-pack was in plain view. It was the biggest pack that Wabi, in all his life in the wilderness, had ever seen, and he mentally figured that there were at least half a hundred animals in it. Like ravenous dogs after having a few scraps of meat flung among them, the wolves were running about, nosing here and there, as if hoping to find a morsel that might have escaped discovery. Then one of them stopped on the trail and, throwing himself half on his haunches, with his head turned to the sky like a baying hound, started the hunt-cry.

"There's two packs. I thought it was too big for one," exclaimed the Indian. "See! Part of them are taking up the trail and the others are lagging behind gnawing the bones of the dead wolf. Now if we only had our ammunition and the other gun those murderers got away from us, we'd make a fortune. What--"

Wabi stopped with a suddenness that spoke volumes, and the supporting arm that he had thrown around Rod's waist tightened until it caused the wounded youth to flinch. Both boys stared in rigid silence. The wolves were crowding around a spot in the snow half-way between the tamarack refuge and the scene of the recent feast. The starved animals betrayed unusual excitement. They had struck the pool of blood and red trail made by the dying moose!

"What is it, Wabi?" whispered Rod.

The Indian did not answer. His black eyes gleamed with a new fire, his lips were parted in anxious anticipation, and he seemed hardly to breathe in his tense interest. The wounded boy repeated his question, and as if in reply the pack swerved to the west and in a black silent mass swept in a direction that would bring them into the tamaracks a hundred yards from the young hunters.

"A new trail!" breathed Wabi. "A new trail, and a hot one! Listen! They make no sound. It is always that way when they are close to a kill!"

As they looked the last of the wolves disappeared in the forest. For a few moments there was silence, then a chorus of howls came from deep in the woods behind them.

"Now is our chance," cried the Indian. "They've broken again, and their game--"

He had partly slipped from his limb, withdrawing his supporting arm from Rod's waist, and was about to descend to the ground when the pack again turned in their direction. A heavy crashing in the underbrush not a dozen rods away sent Wabi in a hurried scramble for his perch.

"Quick--higher up!" he warned excitedly. "They're coming out here--right under us! If we can get up so that they can't see us, or smell us--"

The words were scarcely out of his mouth when a huge shadowy bulk rushed past them not more than fifty feet from the spruce in which they had sought refuge. Both of the boys recognized it as a bull moose, though it did not occur to either of them that it was the same animal at which Wabi had taken a long shot that same day a couple of miles back. In close pursuit came the ravenous pack. Their heads hung close to the bloody trail, hungry, snarling cries coming from between their gaping jaws, they swept across the little opening almost at the young hunters' feet. It was a sight which Rod had never expected to see, and one which held even the more experienced Wabi fascinated. Not a sound fell from either of the youths' lips as they stared down upon the fierce, hungry outlaws of the wilderness. To Wabi this near view of the pack told a fateful story; to Rod it meant nothing more than the tragedy about to be enacted before his eyes. The Indian's keen vision saw in the white moonlight long, thin bodies, starved almost to skin and bone; to his companion the onrushing pack seemed filled only with agile, powerful beasts, maddened to almost fiendish exertions by the nearness of their prey.

In a flash they were gone, but in that moment of their passing there was painted a picture to endure a lifetime in the memory of Roderick Drew. And it was to be followed by one even more tragic, even more thrilling. To the dazed, half-fainting young hunter it seemed but another instant before the pack overhauled the old bull. He saw the doomed monster turn, in the stillness heard the snapping of jaws, the snarling of hunger-crazed animals, and a sound that might have been a great, heaving moan or a dying bellow. In Wabi's veins the blood danced with the excitement that stirred his forefathers to battle. Not a line of the tragedy that was being enacted before his eyes escaped this native son of the wilderness. It was a magnificent fight! He knew that the old bull would die by inches in the one-sided duel, and that when it was over there would be more than one carcass for the survivors to gorge themselves upon. Quietly he reached up and touched his companion.

"Now is our time," he said. "Come on--still--and on this side of the tree!"

He slipped down, foot by foot, assisting Rod as he did so, and when both had reached the ground he bent over as before, that the other might get upon his back.

"I can make it alone, Wabi," whispered the wounded boy. "Give me a lift on the arm, will you?"

With the Indian's arm about his waist, the two set off into the tamaracks. Fifteen minutes later they came to the bank of a small frozen river. On the opposite side of this, a hundred yards down, was a sight which both, as if by a common impulse, welcomed with a glad cry. Close to the shore, sheltered by a dense growth of spruce, was a bright camp-fire. In response to Wabi's far-reaching whoop a shadowy figure appeared in the glow and returned the shout.

"Mukoki!" cried the Indian.

"Mukoki!" laughed Rod, happy that the end was near.

Even as he spoke he swayed dizzily, and Wabi dropped his gun that he might keep his companion from falling into the snow.

CHAPTER II
HOW WABIGOON BECAME A WHITE MAN

Had the young hunters the power of looking into the future, their campfire that night on the frozen Ombabika might have been one of their last, and a few days later would have seen them back on the edges of civilization. Possibly, could they have foreseen the happy culmination of the adventures that lay before them, they would still have gone on, for the love of excitement is strong in the heart of robust youth. But this power of discernment was denied them, and only in after years, with the loved ones of their own firesides close about them, was the whole picture revealed. And in those days, when they would gather with their families about the roaring logs of winter and live over again their early youth, they knew that all the gold in the world would not induce them to part with their memories of the life that had gone before.

A little less than thirty years previous to the time of which we write, a young man named John Newsome left the great city of London for the New World. Fate had played a hard game with young Newsome--had first robbed him of both parents, and then in a single fitful turn of her wheel deprived him of what little property he had inherited. A little later he came to Montreal, and being a youth of good education and considerable ambition, he easily secured a position and worked himself into the confidence of his employers, obtaining an appointment as factor at Wabinosh House, a Post deep in the wilderness of Lake Nipigon.

In the second year of his reign at Wabinosh--a factor is virtually king in his domain--there came to the Post an Indian chief named Wabigoon, and with him his daughter, Minnetaki, in honor of whose beauty and virtue a town was named in after years. Minnetaki was just budding into the early womanhood of her race, and possessed a beauty seldom seen among Indian maidens. If there is such a thing as love at first sight, it sprang into existence the moment John Newsome's eyes fell upon this lovely princess. Thereafter his visits to Wabigoon's village, thirty miles deeper in the wilderness, were of frequent occurrence. From the beginning Minnetaki returned the young factor's affections, but a most potent reason prevented their marriage. For a long time Minnetaki had been ardently wooed by a powerful young chief named Woonga, whom she cordially detested, but upon whose favor and friendship depended the existence of her father's sway over his hunting-grounds.

With the advent of the young factor the bitterest rivalry sprang up between the two suitors, which resulted in two attempts upon Newsome's life, and an ultimatum sent by Woonga to Minnetaki's father. Minnetaki herself replied to this ultimatum. It was a reply that stirred the fires of hatred and revenge to fever heat in Woonga's breast. One dark night, at the head of a score of his tribe, he fell upon Wabigoon's camp, his object being the abduction of the princess. While the attack was successful in a way, its main purpose failed. Wabigoon and a dozen of his tribesmen were slain, but in the end Woonga was driven off.

A swift messenger brought news of the attack and of the old chief's death to Wabinosh House, and with a dozen men Newsome hastened to the assistance of his betrothed and her people. A counter attack was made upon Woonga and he was driven deep into the wilderness with great loss. Three days later Minnetaki became Newsome's wife at the Hudson Bay Post.

From that hour dated one of the most sanguinary feuds in the history of the great trading company; a feud which, as we shall see, was destined to live even unto the second generation.

Woonga and his tribe now became no better than outlaws, and preyed so effectively upon the remnants of the dead Wabigoon's people that the latter were almost exterminated. Those who were left moved to the vicinity of the Post. Hunters from Wabinosh House were ambushed and slain. Indians who came to the Post to trade were regarded as enemies, and the passing of years seemed to make but little difference. The feud still existed. The outlaws came to be spoken of as "Woongas," and a Woonga was regarded as a fair target for any man's rifle.

Meanwhile two children came to bless the happy union of Newsome and his lovely Indian wife. One of these, the eldest, was a boy, and in honor of the old chief he was named Wabigoon, and called Wabi for short. The other was a girl, three years younger, and Newsome insisted that she be called Minnetaki. Curiously enough, the blood of Wabi ran almost pure to his Indian forefathers, while Minnetaki, as she became older, developed less of the wild beauty of her mother and more of the softer loveliness of the white race, her wealth of soft, jet black hair and her great dark eyes contrasting with the lighter skin of her father's blood. Wabi, on the other hand, was an Indian in appearance from his moccasins to the crown of his head, swarthy, sinewy, as agile as a lynx, and with every instinct in him crying for the life of the wild. Yet born in him was a Caucasian shrewdness and intelligence that reached beyond the factor himself.

One of Newsome's chief pleasures in life had been the educating of his woodland bride, and it was the ambition of both that the little Minnetaki and her brother be reared in the ways of white children. Consequently both mother and father began their education at the Post; they were sent to the factor's school and two winters were passed in Port Arthur that they might have the advantage of thoroughly equipped schools. The children proved themselves unusually bright pupils, and by the time Wabi was sixteen and Minnetaki twelve one would not have known from their manner of speech that Indian blood ran in their veins. Yet both, by the common desire of their parents, were familiar with the life of the Indian and could talk fluently the tongue of their mother's people.

It was at about this time in their lives that the Woongas became especially daring in their depredations. These outlaws no longer pretended to earn their livelihood by honest means, but preyed upon trappers and other Indians without discrimination, robbing and killing whenever safe opportunities offered themselves. The hatred for the people of Wabinosh House became hereditary, and the Woonga children grew up with it in their hearts. The real cause of the feud had been forgotten by many, though not by Woonga himself. At last so daring did he become that the provincial government placed a price upon his head and upon those of a number of his most notorious followers. For a time the outlaws were driven from the country, but the bloodthirsty chief himself could not be captured.

When Wabi was seventeen years of age it was decided that he should be sent to some big school in the States for a year. Against this plan the young Indian--nearly all people regarded him as an Indian, and Wabi was proud of the fact--fought with all of the arguments at his command. He loved the wilds with the passion of his mother's race. His nature revolted at the thoughts of a great city with its crowded streets, its noise, and bustle, and dirt. It was then that Minnetaki pleaded with him, begged him to go for just one year, and to come back and tell her of all he had seen and teach her what he had learned. Wabi loved his beautiful little sister beyond anything else on earth, and it was she more than his parents who finally induced him to go.

For three months Wabi devoted himself faithfully to his studies in Detroit. But each week added to his loneliness and his longings for Minnetaki and his forests. The passing of each day became a painful task to him. To Minnetaki he wrote three times each week, and three times each week the little maiden at Wabinosh House wrote long, cheering letters to her brother--though they came to Wabi only about twice a month, because only so often did the mail-carrier go out from the Post.

It was at this time in his lonely school life that Wabigoon became acquainted with Roderick Drew. Roderick, even as Wabi fancied himself to be just at this time, was a child of misfortune. His father had died before he could remember, and the property he had left had dwindled slowly away during the passing of years. Rod was spending his last week in school when he met Wabigoon. Necessity had become his grim master, and the following week he was going to work. As the boy described the situation to his Indian friend, his mother "had fought to the last ditch to keep him in school, but now his time was up." Wabi seized upon the white youth as an oasis in a vast desert. After a little the two became almost inseparable, and their friendship culminated in Wabi's going to live in the Drew home. Mrs. Drew was a woman of education and refinement, and her interest in Wabigoon was almost that of a mother. In this environment the ragged edges were smoothed away from the Indian boy's deportment, and his letters to Minnetaki were more and more filled with enthusiastic descriptions of his new friends. After a little Mrs. Drew received a grateful letter of thanks from the princess mother at Wabinosh House, and thus a pleasant correspondence sprang up between the two.

There were now few lonely hours for the two boys. During the long winter evenings, when Roderick was through with his day's work and Wabi had completed his studies, they would sit before the fire and the Indian youth would describe the glorious life of the vast northern wilderness; and day by day, and week by week, there steadily developed within Rod's breast a desire to see and live that life. A thousand plans were made, a thousand adventures pictured, and the mother would smile and laugh and plan with them.

But in time the end of it all came, and Wabi went back to the princess mother, to Minnetaki, and to his forests. There were tears in the boys' eyes when they parted, and the mother cried for the Indian boy who was returning to his people. Many of the days that followed were painful to Roderick Drew. Eight months had bred a new nature in him, and when Wabi left it was as if a part of his own life had gone with him. Spring came and passed, and then summer. Every mail from Wabinosh House brought letters for the Drews, and never did an Indian courier drop a pack at the Post that did not carry a bundle of letters for Wabigoon.

Then in the early autumn, when September frosts were turning the leaves of the North to red and gold, there came the long letter from Wabi which brought joy, excitement and misgiving into the little home of the mother and her son. It was accompanied by one from the factor himself, another from the princess mother, and by a tiny note from Minnetaki, who pleaded with the others that Roderick and Mrs. Drew might spend the winter with them at Wabinosh House.

"You need not fear about losing your position." wrote Wabigoon. "We shall make more money up here this winter than you could earn in Detroit in three years. We will hunt wolves. The country is alive with them, and the government gives a bounty of fifteen dollars for every scalp taken. Two winters ago I killed forty and I did not make a business of it at that. I have a tame wolf which we use as a decoy. Don't bother about a gun or anything like that. We have everything here."

For several days Mrs. Drew and her son deliberated upon the situation before a reply was sent to the Newsomes. Roderick pleaded, pictured the glorious times they would have, the health that it would give them, and marshaled in a dozen different ways his arguments in favor of accepting the invitation. On the other hand, his mother was filled with doubt. Their finances were alarmingly low, and Rod would be giving up a sure though small income, which was now supporting them comfortably. His future was bright, and that winter would see him promoted to ten dollars a week in the mercantile house where he was employed. In the end they came to an understanding. Mrs. Drew would not go to Wabinosh House, but she would allow Roderick to spend the winter there--and word to this effect was sent off into the wilderness.

Three weeks later came Wabigoon's reply. On the tenth of October he would meet Rod at Sprucewood, on the Black Sturgeon River. Thence they would travel by canoe up the Sturgeon River to Sturgeon Lake, take portage to Lake Nipigon, and arrive at Wabinosh House before the ice of early winter shut them in. There was little time to lose in making preparations, and the fourth day following the receipt of Wabi's letter found Rod and his mother waiting for the train which was to whirl the boy into his new life. Not until the eleventh did he arrive at Sprucewood. Wabi was there to meet him, accompanied by an Indian from the Post; and that same afternoon the journey up Black Sturgeon River was begun.

CHAPTER III
RODERICK SEES THE FOOTPRINT

Rod was now plunged for the first time in his life into the heart of the Wilderness. Seated in the bow of the birch-bark canoe which was carrying them up the Sturgeon, with Wabi close behind him, he drank in the wild beauties of the forests and swamps through which they slipped almost as noiselessly as shadows, his heart thumping in joyous excitement, his eyes constantly on the alert for signs of the big game which Wabi told him was on all sides of them. Across his knees, ready for instant use, was Wabi's repeating rifle. The air was keen with the freshness left by night frosts. At times deep masses of gold and crimson forests shut them in, at others, black forests of spruce came down to the river's edge; again they would pass silently through great swamps of tamaracks. In this vast desolation there was a mysterious quiet, except for the occasional sounds of wild life. Partridges drummed back in the woods, flocks of ducks got up with a great rush of wings at almost every turn, and once, late in the morning of the first day out, Rod was thrilled by a crashing in the undergrowth scarcely a stone's throw from the canoe. He could see saplings twisting and bending, and heard Wabi whisper behind him:

"A moose!"

They were words to set his hands trembling and his whole body quivering with anticipation. There was in him now none of the old hunter's coolness, none of the almost stoical indifference with which the men of the big North hear these sounds of the wild things about them. Rod had yet to see his first big game.

That moment came in the afternoon. The canoe had skimmed lightly around a bend in the river. Beyond this bend a mass of dead driftwood had wedged against the shore, and this driftwood, as the late sun sank behind the forests, was bathed in a warm yellow glow. And basking in this glow, as he loves to do at the approach of winter nights, was an animal, the sight of which drew a sharp, excited cry from between Rod's lips. In an instant he had recognized it as a bear. The animal was taken completely by surprise and was less than half a dozen rods away. Quick as a flash, and hardly realizing what he was doing, the boy drew his rifle to his shoulder, took quick aim and fired. The bear was already clambering up the driftwood, but stopped suddenly at the report, slipped as if about to fall back--then continued his retreat.

"You hit 'im!" shouted Wabi. "Quick-try 'im again!"

Rod's second shot seemed to have no effect In his excitement he jumped to his feet, forgetting that he was in a frail canoe, and took a last shot at the big black beast that was just about to disappear over the edge of the driftwood. Both Wabi and his Indian companion flung themselves on the shore side of their birch and dug their paddles deep into the water, but their efforts were unavailing to save their reckless comrade. Unbalanced by the concussion of his gun, Rod plunged backward into the river, but before he had time to sink, Wabi reached over and grabbed him by the arm.

"Don't make a move--and hang on to the gun!" he warned. "If we try to get you in here we'll all go over!" He made a sign to the Indian, who swung the canoe slowly inshore. Then he grinned down into Rod's dripping, unhappy face.

"By George, that last shot was a dandy for a tenderfoot! You got your bear!"

Despite his uncomfortable position, Rod gave a whoop of joy, and no sooner did his feet touch solid bottom than he loosened himself from Wabi's grip and plunged toward the driftwood. On its very top he found the bear, as dead as a bullet through its side and another through its head could make it. Standing there beside his first big game, dripping and shivering, he looked down upon the two who were pulling their canoe ashore and gave, a series of triumphant whoops that could have been heard half a mile away.

"It's camp and a fire for you," laughed Wabi, hurrying up to him. "This is better luck than I thought you'd have, Rod. We'll have a glorious feast to-night, and a fire of this driftwood that will show you what makes life worth the living up here in the North. Ho, Muky," he called to the old Indian, "cut this fellow up, will you? I'll make camp."

"Can we keep the skin?" asked Rod. "It's my first, you know, and--"

"Of course we can. Give us a hand with the fire, Rod; it will keep you from catching cold."

In the excitement of making their first camp, Rod almost forgot that he was soaked to the skin, and that night was falling about them. The first step was the building of a fire, and soon a great, crackling, almost smokeless blaze was throwing its light and heat for thirty feet around. Wabi now brought blankets from the canoe, stripped off a part of his own clothes, made Rod undress, and soon had that youth swathed in dry togs, while his wet ones were hung close up to the fire. For the first time Rod saw the making of a wilderness shelter. Whistling cheerily, Wabi got an ax from the canoe, went into the edge of the cedars and cut armful after armful of saplings and boughs. Tying his blankets about himself, Rod helped to carry these, a laughable and grotesque figure as he stumbled about clumsily in his efforts. Within half an hour the cedar shelter was taking form. Two crotched saplings were driven into the ground eight feet apart, and from one to the other, resting in the crotches, was placed another sapling, which formed the ridge-pole; and from this pole there ran slantwise to the earth half a dozen others, making a framework upon which the cedar boughs were piled. By the time the old Indian had finished his bear the home was completed, and with its beds of sweet-smelling boughs, the great camp-fire in front and the dense wilderness about them growing black with the approach of night, Rod thought that nothing in picture-book or story could quite equal the reality of that moment. And when, a few moments later, great bear-steaks were broiling over a mass of coals, and the odor of coffee mingled with that of meal-cakes sizzling on a heated stone, he knew that his dearest dreams had come true.

That night in the glow of the camp-fire Rod listened to the thrilling stories of Wabi and the old Indian, and lay awake until nearly dawn, listening to the occasional howl of a wolf, mysterious splashings in the river and the shrill notes of the night birds. There were varied experiences in the following three days: one frosty morning before the others were awake he stole out from the camp with Wabi's rifle and shot twice at a red deer--which he missed both times; there was an exciting but fruitless race with a swimming caribou in Sturgeon Lake, at which Wabi himself took three long-range shots without effect.

It was on a glorious autumn afternoon that Wabi's keen eyes first descried the log buildings of the Post snuggled in the edge of the seemingly unending forest. As they approached he joyfully pointed out the different buildings to Rod--the Company store, the little cluster of employees' homes and the factor's house, where Rod was to meet his welcome. At least Roderick himself had thought it would be there. But as they came nearer a single canoe shot out suddenly from the shore and the young hunters could see a white handkerchief waving them greeting. Wabi replied with a whoop of pleasure and fired his gun into the air.

"It's Minnetaki!" he cried. "She said she would watch for us and come out to meet us!"

Minnetaki! A little nervous thrill shot through Rod. Wabi had described her to him a thousand times in those winter evenings at home; with a brother's love and pride he had always brought her into their talks and plans, and somehow, little by little, Rod had grown to like her very much without ever having seen her.

The two canoes swiftly approached each other, and in a few minutes more were alongside. With a glad laughing cry Minnetaki leaned over and kissed her brother, while at the same time her dark eyes shot a curious glance at the youth of whom she had read and heard so much.

At this time Minnetaki was fifteen. Like her mother's race she was slender, of almost woman's height, and unconsciously as graceful as a fawn in her movements. A slightly waving wealth of raven hair framed what Rod thought to be one of the prettiest faces he had ever seen, and entwined in the heavy silken braid that fell over her shoulder were a number of red autumn leaves. As she straightened herself in her canoe she looked at Rod and smiled, and he in making a polite effort to lift his cap in civilized style, lost that article of apparel in a sudden gust of wind. In an instant there was a general laugh of merriment in which even the old Indian joined. The little incident did more toward making comradeship than anything else that might have happened, and laughing again into Rod's face Minnetaki urged her canoe toward the floating cap.

"You shouldn't wear such things until it gets cold," she said, after retrieving the cap and handing it to him. "Wabi does--but I don't!"

"Then I won't," replied Rod gallantly, and at Wabi's burst of laughter both blushed.

That first night at the Post Rod found that Wabi had already made all plans for the winter's hunting, and the white youth's complete equipment was awaiting him in the room assigned to him in the factor's house--a deadly looking five-shot Remington, similar to Wabi's, a long-barreled, heavy-caliber revolver, snow-shoes, and a dozen other articles necessary to one about to set out upon a long expedition in the wilderness. Wabi had also mapped out their hunting-grounds. Wolves in the immediate neighborhood of the Post, where they were being constantly sought by the Indians and the factor's men, had become exceedingly cautious and were not numerous, but in the almost untraveled wilderness a hundred miles to the north and east they were literally overrunning the country, killing moose, caribou and deer in great numbers.

In this region Wabi planned to make their winter quarters. And no time was to be lost in taking up the trail, for the log house in which they would pass the bitterly cold months should be built before the heavy snows set in. It was therefore decided that the young hunters should start within a week, accompanied by Mukoki, the old Indian, a cousin of the slain Wabigoon, whom Wabi had given the nickname of Muky and who had been a faithful comrade to him from his earliest childhood.

Rod made the most of the six days which were allotted to him at the Post, and while Wabi helped to handle the affairs of the Company's store during a short absence of his father at Port Arthur, the lovely little Minnetaki gave our hero his first lessons in woodcraft. In canoe, with the rifle, and in reading the signs of forest life Wabi's sister awakened constantly increasing admiration in Rod. To see her bending over some freshly made trail, her cheeks flushed, her eyes sparkling with excitement, her rich hair filled with the warmth of the sun, was a picture to arouse enthusiasm even in the heart of a youngster of eighteen, and a hundred times the boy mentally vowed that "she was a brick" from the tips of her pretty moccasined feet to the top of her prettier head. Half a dozen times at least he voiced this sentiment to Wabi, and Wabi agreed with great enthusiasm. In fact, by the time the week was almost gone Minnetaki and Rod had become great chums, and it was not without some feeling of regret that the young wolf hunter greeted the dawn of the day that was to see them begin their journey deeper into the wilds.

Minnetaki was one of the earliest risers at the Post. Rod was seldom behind her. But on this particular morning he was late and heard the girl whistling outside half an hour before he was dressed--for Minnetaki could whistle in a manner that often filled him with envy. By the time he came down she had disappeared in the edge of the forest, and Wabi, who was also ahead of him, was busy with Mukoki tying up their equipment in packs. It was a glorious morning, clear and frosty, and Rod noticed that a thin shell of ice had formed on the lake during the night. Once or twice Wabi turned toward the forest and gave his signal whoop, but received no reply.

"I don't see why Minnetaki doesn't come back," he remarked carelessly, as he fastened a shoulder-strap about a bundle. "Breakfast will be ready in a jiffy. Hunt her up, will you, Rod?"

Nothing loath, Rod started out on a brisk run along the path which he knew to be a favorite with Minnetaki and shortly it brought him down to a pebbly stretch of the beach where she frequently left her canoe. That she had been here a few minutes before he could tell by the fact that the ice about the birch-bark was broken, as though the girl had tested its thickness by shoving the light craft out into it for a few feet. Her footsteps led plainly up the shelving shore and into the forest.

"O Minnetaki--Minnetaki!"

Rod called loudly and listened. There was no response. As if impelled by some presentiment which he himself could not explain, the boy hurried deeper into the forest along the narrow path which Minnetaki must have taken. Five minutes--ten minutes--and he called again. Still there was no answer. Possibly the girl had not gone so far, or she might have left the path for the thick woods. A little farther on there was a soft spot in the path where a great tree-trunk had rotted half a century before, leaving a rich black soil. Clearly traced in this were the imprints of Minnetaki's moccasins. For a full minute Rod stopped and listened, making not a sound. Why he maintained silence he could not have explained. But he knew that he was half a mile from the Post, and that Wabi's sister should not be here at breakfast time. In this minute's quiet he unconsciously studied the tracks in the ground. How small the pretty Indian maiden's feet were! And he noticed, too, that her moccasins, unlike most moccasins, had a slight heel.

But in a moment more his inspection was cut short. Was that a cry he heard far ahead? His heart seemed to stop beating, his blood thrilled--and in another instant he was running down the path like a deer. Twenty rods beyond this point the path entered an opening in the forest made by a great fire, and half-way across this opening the youth saw a sight which chilled him to the marrow. There was Minnetaki, her long hair tumbling loosely down her back, a cloth tied around her head--and on either side an Indian dragging her swiftly toward the opposite forest!

For as long as he might have drawn three breaths Rod stood transfixed with horror. Then his senses returned to him, and every muscle in his body seemed to bound with action. For days he had been practising with his revolver and it was now in the holster at his side. Should he use it? Or might he hit Minnetaki? At his feet he saw a club and snatching this up he sped across the opening, the soft earth holding the sound of his steps. When he was a dozen feet behind the Indians Minnetaki stumbled in a sudden effort to free herself, and as one of her captors half turned to drag her to her feet he saw the enraged youth, club uplifted, bearing down upon them like a demon. A terrific yell from Rod, a warning cry from the Indian, and the fray began. With crushing force, the boy's club fell upon the shoulder of the second Indian, and before he could recover from the delivery of this blow the youth was caught in a choking, deadly grip by the other from behind.

Freed by the sudden attack, Minnetaki tore away the cloth that bound her eyes and mouth. As quick as a flash she took in the situation. At her feet the wounded Indian was half rising, and upon the ground near him, struggling in close embrace, were Rod and the other. She saw the Indian's fatal grip upon her preserver's throat, the whitening face and wide-open eyes, and with a great, sobbing cry she caught up the fallen club and brought it down with all her strength upon the redskin's head. Twice, three times the club rose and fell, and the grip on Rod's throat relaxed. A fourth time it rose, but this time was caught from behind, and a huge hand clutched the brave girl's throat so that the cry on her lips died in a gasp. But the relief gave Rod his opportunity. With a tremendous effort he reached his pistol holster, drew out the gun, and pressed it close up against his assailant's body. There was a muffled report and with a shriek of agony the Indian pitched backward. Hearing the shot and seeing the effect upon his comrade, the second Indian released his hold on Minnetaki and ran for the forest. Rod, seeing Minnetaki fall in a sobbing, frightened heap, forgot all else but to run to her, smooth back her hair and comfort her with all of the assurances at his boyish command.

It was here that Wabi and the old Indian guide found them five minutes later. Hearing Rod's first piercing yell of attack, they had raced into the forest, afterward guided by the two or three shrill screams which Minnetaki had unconsciously emitted during the struggle. Close behind them, smelling trouble, followed two of the Post employees.

The attempted abduction of Wabi's sister, Rod's heroic rescue and the death of one of the captors, who was recognized as one of Woonga's men, caused a seven-day sensation at the Post.

There was now no thought of leaving on the part of the young wolf hunters. It was evident that Woonga was again in the neighborhood, and Wabi and Rod, together with a score of Indians and hunters, spent days in scouring the forests and swamps. But the Woongas disappeared as suddenly as they came. Not until Wabi had secured a promise from Minnetaki that she would no longer go into the forests unaccompanied did the Indian youth again allow himself to take up their interrupted plans.

Minnetaki had been within easy calling distance of help when the Woongas, without warning, sprang upon her, smothered her attempted cries and dragged her away, compelling her to walk alone over the soft earth where Rod had seen her footsteps, so that any person who followed might suppose she was alone and safe. This fact stirred the dozen white families at the Post into aggressive action, and four of the most skillful Indian track-hunters in the service were detailed to devote themselves exclusively to hunting down the outlaws, their operations not to include a territory extending more than twenty miles from Wabinosh House in any direction. With these precautions it was believed that no harm could come to Minnetaki or other young girls of the Post.

It was, therefore, on a Monday, the fourth day of November, that Rod, Wabi and Mukoki turned their faces at last to the adventures that awaited them in the great North.

CHAPTER IV
RODERICK'S FIRST TASTE OF THE HUNTER'S LIFE

By this time it was bitter cold. The lakes and rivers were frozen deep and a light snow covered the ground. Already two weeks behind their plans, the young wolf hunters and the old Indian made forced marches around the northern extremity of Lake Nipigon and on the sixth day found themselves on the Ombabika River, where they were compelled to stop on account of a dense snow-storm. A temporary camp was made, and it was while constructing this camp that Mukoki discovered signs of wolves. It was therefore decided to remain for a day or two and investigate the hunting-grounds. On the morning of the second day Wabi shot at and wounded the old bull moose which met such a tragic end a few hours later, and that same morning the two boys made a long tour to the north in the hope of finding that they were in a good game country, which would mean also that there were plenty of wolves.

This left Mukoki alone in camp. Thus far, in their desire to cover as much ground as possible before the heavy snows came, Wabi and his companions had not stopped to hunt for game and for six days their only meat had been bacon and jerked venison. Mukoki, whose prodigious appetite was second only to the shrewdness with which he stalked game to satisfy it, determined to add to their larder if possible during the others' absence, and with this object in view he left camp late in the afternoon to be gone, as he anticipated, not longer than an hour or so.

With him he carried two powerful wolf-traps slung over his shoulders. Stealing cautiously along the edge of the river, his eyes and ears alert for game, Mukoki suddenly came upon the frozen and half-eaten carcass of a red deer. It was evident that the animal had been killed by wolves either the day or night before, and from the tracks in the snow the Indian concluded that not more than four wolves had participated in the slaughter and feast. That these wolves would return to continue their banquet, probably that night, Mukoki's many experiences as a wolf hunter assured him; and he paused long enough to set his traps, afterward covering them over with three or four inches of snow.

Continuing his hunt, the old Indian soon struck the fresh spoor of a deer. Believing that the animal would not travel for any great distance in the deep snow, he swiftly took up the trail. Half a mile farther on he stopped abruptly with a grunt of unbounded surprise. Another hunter had taken up the trail!

With increased caution Mukoki now advanced. Two hundred feet more and a second pair of moccasined feet joined in the pursuit, and a little later still a third!

Led on by curiosity more than by the hope of securing a partnership share in the quarry, the Indian slipped silently and swiftly through the forest. As he emerged from a dense growth of spruce through which the tracks led him Mukoki was treated to another surprise by almost stumbling over the carcass of the deer he had been following. A brief examination satisfied him that the doe had been shot at least two hours before. The three hunters had cut out her heart, liver and tongue and had also taken the hind quarters, leaving the remainder of the carcass and the skin! Why had they neglected this most valuable part of their spoils? With a new gleam of interest in his eyes Mukoki carefully scrutinized the moccasin trails. He soon discovered that the Indians ahead of him were in great haste, and that after cutting the choicest meat from the doe they had started off to make up for lost time by running!

With another grunt of astonishment the old Indian returned to the carcass, quickly stripped off the skin, wrapped in it the fore quarters and ribs of the doe, and thus loaded, took up the home trail. It was dark when he reached camp. Wabi and Rod had not yet returned. Building a huge fire and hanging the ribs of the doe on a spit before it, he anxiously awaited their appearance.

Half an hour later he heard the shout which brought him quickly to where Wabi was holding the partly unconscious form of Rod in his arms.

It took but a few moments to carry the injured youth to camp, and not until Rod was resting upon a pile of blankets in their shack, with the warmth of the fire reviving him, did Wabi vouchsafe an explanation to the old Indian.

"I guess he's got a broken arm, Muky," he said. "Have you any hot water?"

"Shot?" asked the old hunter, paying no attention to the question. He dropped upon his knees beside Rod, his long brown fingers reaching out anxiously. "Shot?"

"No--hit with a club. We met three Indian hunters who were in camp and who invited us to eat with them. While we were eating they jumped upon our backs. Rod got that--and lost his rifle!"

Mukoki quickly stripped the wounded boy of his garments, baring his left arm and side. The arm was swollen and almost black and there was a great bruise on Rod's body a little above the waist. Mukoki was a surgeon by necessity, a physician such as one finds only in the vast unblazed wildernesses, where Nature is the teacher. Crudely he made his examination, pinching and twisting the flesh and bones until Rod cried out in pain, but in the end there was a glad triumph in his voice as he said:

"No bone broke--hurt most here!" and he touched the bruise. "Near broke rib--not quite. Took wind out and made great deal sick. Want good supper, hot coffee--rub in bear's grease, then be better!"

Rod, who had opened his eyes, smiled faintly and Wabi gave a half-shout of delight.

"Not so bad as we thought, eh, Rod?" he cried. "You can't fool Muky! If he says your arm isn't broken--why, it *isn't*, and that's all there is to it. Let me bolster you up in these blankets and we'll soon have a supper that will sizzle the aches out of you. I smell meat--fresh meat!"

With a chuckle of pleasure Mukoki jumped to his feet and ran out to where the ribs of the doe were slowly broiling over the fire. They were already done to a rich brown and their dripping juice filled the nostrils with an appetizing odor. By the time Wabi had applied Mukoki's prescription to his comrade's wounds, and had done them up in bandages, the tempting feast was spread before them.

As a liberal section of the ribs was placed before him, together with corn-meal cakes and a cup of steaming coffee, Rod could not suppress a happy though somewhat embarrassed laugh.

"I'm ashamed of myself, Wabi," he said. "Here I've been causing so much bother, like some helpless kid; and now I find I haven't even the excuse of a broken arm, and that I'm as hungry as a bear! Looks pretty yellow, doesn't it? Just as though I was scared to death! So help me, I almost wish my arm *was* broken!"

Mukoki had buried his teeth in a huge chunk of fat rib, but he lowered it with a great chuckling grunt, half of his face smeared with the first results of his feast.

"Whole lot sick," he explained. "Be sick some more--mighty sick! Maybe vomit lots!"

"Waugh!" shrieked Wabi. "How is that for cheerful news, Rod?" His merriment echoed far out into the night. Suddenly he caught himself and peered suspiciously into the gloom beyond the circle of firelight.

"Do you suppose they would follow?" he asked.

A more cautious silence followed, and the Indian youth quickly related the adventures of the day to Mukoki--how, in the heart of the forest several miles beyond the lake, they had come upon the Indian hunters, had accepted of their seemingly honest hospitality, and in the midst of their meal had suffered an attack from them. So sudden and unexpected had been the assault that one of the Indians got away with Rod's rifle, ammunition belt and revolver before any effort could be made to stop him. Wabi was under the other two Indians when Rod came to his assistance, with the result that the latter was struck two heavy blows, either with a club or a gun-stock. So tenaciously had the Indian boy clung to his own weapon that his assailants, after a brief struggle, darted into the dense underbrush, evidently satisfied with the white boy's equipment.

"They were of Woonga's people, without a doubt," finished Wabi. "It puzzles me why they didn't kill us. They had half a dozen chances to shoot us, but didn't seem to want to do us any great injury. Either the measures taken at the Post are making them reform, or--"

He paused, a troubled look in his eyes. Immediately Mukoki told of his own experience and of the mysterious haste of the three Indians who had slain the doe.

"It is certainly curious," rejoined the young Indian. "They couldn't have been the ones we met, but I'll wager they belong to the same gang. I wouldn't be surprised if we had hit upon one of Woonga's retreats. We've always thought he was in the Thunder Bay regions to the west, and that is where father is watching for him now. We've hit the hornets' nest, Muky, and the only thing for us to do is to get out of this country as fast as we can!"

"We'd make a nice pot-shot just at this moment," volunteered Rod, looking across to the dense blackness on the opposite side of the river, where the moonlight seemed to make even more impenetrable the wall of gloom.

As he spoke there came a slight sound from behind him, the commotion of a body moving softly beyond the wall of spruce boughs, then a curious, suspicious sniffing, and after that a low whine.

"Listen!"

Wabi's command came in a tense whisper. He leaned close against the boughs, stealthily parted them, and slowly thrust his head through the aperture.

"Hello, Wolf!" he whispered. "What's up?"

An arm's length away, tied before a smaller shelter of spruce, a gaunt, dog-like animal stood in a rigid listening attitude. An instant's glance, however, would have assured one that it was not a dog, but a full-grown wolf. From the days of its puppyhood Wabi had taught it in the ways of dogdom, yet had the animal perversely clung to its wild instincts. A weakness in that thong, a slip of the collar, and Wolf would have bounded joyously into the forests to seek for ever the packs of his fathers. Now the babeesh rope was taut, Wolf's muzzle was turned half to the sky, his ears were alert, half-sounding notes rattled in his throat.

"There is something near our camp!" announced the Indian boy, drawing himself back quickly. "Muky--"

He was interrupted by a long mournful howl from the captive wolf.

Mukoki had jumped to his feet with the alertness of a cat, and now with his gun in his hand slunk around the edge of the shelter and buried himself in the gloom. Roderick lay quiet while Wabi, seizing the remaining rifle, followed him.

"Lie over there in the dark, Rod, where the firelight doesn't show you up," he cautioned in a low voice. "Probably it is only some animal that has stumbled on to our camp, but we want to make sure."

Ten minutes later the young hunter returned alone.

"False alarm!" he laughed cheerfully. "There's a part of a carcass of a red deer up the creek a bit. It has been killed by wolves, and Wolf smells some of his own blood coming in to the feast. Muky has set traps there and we may have our first scalp in the morning."

"Where is Mukoki?"

"On watch. He is going to keep guard until a little after midnight, and then I'll turn out. We can't be too careful, with the Woongas in the neighborhood."

Rod shifted himself uneasily.

"What shall we do--to-morrow?" he asked.

"Get out!" replied Wabi with emphasis. "That is, if you are able to travel. From what Mukoki tells me, and from what you and I already know, Woonga's people must be in the forests beyond the lake. We'll cut a trail up the Ombabika for two or three days before we strike camp. You and Muky can start out as soon as it is light enough."

"And you--" began Rod.

"Oh, I'm going to take a run back over our old wolf-trail and collect the scalps we shot to-day. There's a month's salary back there for you, Rod! Now, let's turn in. Good night--sleep tight--and be sure to wake up early in the morning."

The boys, exhausted by the adventures of the day, were soon in profound slumber. And though midnight came, and hour after hour passed between then and dawn, the faithful Mukoki did not awaken them. Never for a moment neglecting his caution the old Indian watched tirelessly over the camp. With the first appearance of day he urged the fire into a roaring blaze, raked out a great mass of glowing coals, and proceeded to get breakfast. Wabi discovered him at this task when he awoke from his slumber.

"I didn't think you would play this trick on me, Muky," he said, a flush of embarrassment gathering in his brown face. "It's awfully good of you, and all that, but I wish you wouldn't treat me as if I were a child any longer, old friend!"

He placed his hand affectionately upon the kneeling Mukoki's shoulder, and the old hunter looked up at him with a happy, satisfied grin on his weather-beaten visage, wrinkled and of the texture of leather by nearly fifty years of life in the wilderness. It was Mukoki who had first carried the baby Wabi about the woods upon his shoulders; it was he who had played with him, cared for him, and taught him in the ways of the wild in early childhood, and it was he who had missed him most, with little Minnetaki, when he went away to school. All the love in the grim old redskin's heart was for the Indian youth and his sister, and to them Mukoki was a second father, a silent, watchful guardian and comrade. This one loving touch of Wabi's hand was ample reward for the long night's duty, and his pleasure expressed itself in two or three low chuckling grunts.

"Had heap bad day," he replied. "Very much tired. Me feel good--better than sleep!" He rose to his feet and handed Wabi the long fork with which he manipulated the meat on the spits. "You can tend to that," he added. "I go see traps."

Rod, who had awakened and overheard these last remarks, called out from the shack:

"Wait a minute, Mukoki. I'm going with you. If you've got a wolf, I want to see him."

"Got one sure 'nuff," grinned the old Indian.

In a few minutes Rod came out, fully dressed and with a much healthier color in his face than when he went to bed the preceding night. He stood before the fire, stretched one arm then the other, gave a slight grimace of pain, and informed his anxious comrades that he seemed to be as well as ever, except that his arm and side were very sore.

Walking slowly, that Rod might "find himself," as Wabi expressed it, the two went up the river. It was a dull gray morning and occasionally large flakes of snow fell, giving evidence that before the day was far advanced another storm would set in. Mukoki's traps were not more than an eighth of a mile from camp, and as the two rounded a certain bend in the river the old hunter suddenly stopped with a huge grant of satisfaction. Following the direction in which he pointed Rod saw a dark object lying in the snow a short distance away.

"That's heem!" exclaimed the Indian.

As they approached, the object became animate, pulling and tearing in the snow as though in the agonies of death. A few moments more and they were close up to the captive.

"She wolf!" explained Mukoki.

He gripped the ax he had brought with him and approached within a few feet of the crouching animal. Rod could see that one of the big steel traps had caught the wolf on the forward leg and that the other had buried its teeth in one of the hind legs. Thus held the doomed animal could make little effort to protect itself and crouched in sullen quiet, its white fangs gleaming in a noiseless, defiant snarl, its eyes shining with pain and anger, and with only its thin starved body, which jerked and trembled as the Indian came nearer, betraying signs of fear. To Rod it might have been a pitiful sight had not there come to him a thought of the preceding night and of his own and Wabi's narrow escape from the pack.

Two or three quick blows of the ax and the wolf was dead. With a skill which can only be found among those of his own race, Mukoki drew his knife, cut deftly around the wolf's head just below the ears, and with one downward, one upward, and two sidewise jerks tore off the scalp.

Suddenly, without giving a thought to his speech, there shot from Rod,

"Is that the way you scalp people?"

Mukoki looked up, his jaw fell--and then he gave the nearest thing to a real laugh that Rod ever heard come from between his lips. When Mukoki laughed it was usually in a half-chuckle, a half-gurgle--something that neither Rod nor Wabi could have imitated if they had tried steadily for a month.

"Never scalped white people," the old Indian shot back. "Father did when-- young man. Did great scalp business!"

Mukoki had not done chuckling to himself even when they reached camp.

Scarcely ten minutes were taken in eating breakfast. Snow was already beginning to fall, and if the hunters took up their trail at once their tracks would undoubtedly be entirely obliterated by midday, which was the best possible thing that could happen for them in the Woonga country. On the other hand, Wabi was anxious to follow back over the wolf-trail before the snow shut it in. There was no danger of their becoming separated and lost, for it was agreed that Rod and Mukoki should travel straight up the frozen river. Wabi would overtake them before nightfall.

Arming himself with his rifle, revolver, knife, and a keen-edged belt-ax, the Indian boy lost no time in leaving camp. A quarter of an hour later Wabi came out cautiously on the end of the lake where had occurred the unequal duel between the old bull moose and the wolves. A single glance told him what the outcome of that duel had been. Twenty rods out upon the snow he saw parts of a great skeleton, and a huge pair of antlers.

As he stood on the arena of the mighty battle, Wabi would have given a great deal if Rod could have been with him. There lay the heroic old moose, now nothing more than a skeleton. But the magnificent head and horns still remained--the largest head that the Indian youth, in all his wilderness life, had ever seen--and it occurred to him that if this head could be preserved and taken back to civilization it would be worth a hundred dollars or more. That the old bull had put up a magnificent fight was easily discernible. Fifty feet away were the bones of a wolf, and almost under the skeleton of the moose were those of another. The heads of both still remained, and Wabi, after taking their scalps, hurried on over the trail.

Half-way across the lake, where he had taken his last two shots, were the skeletons of two more wolves, and in the edge of the spruce forest he found another. This animal had evidently been wounded farther back and had later been set upon by some of the pack and killed. Half a mile deeper in the forest he came upon a spot where he had emptied five shells into the pack and here he found the bones of two more wolves. He had seven scalps in his possession when he turned back over the home trail.

Beside the remains of the old bull Wabi paused again. He knew that the Indians frequently preserved moose and caribou heads through the winter by keeping them frozen, and the head at his feet was a prize worth some thought. But how could he keep it preserved until their return, months later? He could not suspend it from the limb of a tree, as was the custom when in camp, for it would either be stolen by some passing hunter or spoiled by the first warm days of spring. Suddenly an idea came to him. Why could it not be preserved in what white hunters called an "Indian ice-box"? In an instant he was acting upon this inspiration. It was not a small task to drag the huge head to the shelter of the tamaracks, where, safely hidden from view, he made a closer examination. The head was gnawed considerably by the wolves, but Wabi had seen worse ones skillfully repaired by the Indians at the Post.

Under a dense growth of spruce, where the rays of the sun seldom penetrated, the Indian boy set to work with his belt-ax. For an hour and a half he worked steadily, and at the end of that time had dug a hole in the frozen earth three feet deep and four feet square. This hole he now lined with about two inches of snow, packed as tight as he could jam it with the butt of his gun. Then placing in the head he packed snow closely about it and afterward filled in the earth, stamping upon the hard chunks with his feet. When all was done he concealed the signs of his work under a covering of snow, blazed two trees with his ax, and resumed his journey.

"There is thirty dollars for each of us if there's a cent," he mused softly, as he hurried toward the Ombabika. "That ground won't thaw out until June. A moose-head and eight scalps at fifteen dollars each isn't bad for one day's work, Rod, old boy!"

He had been absent for three hours. It had been snowing steadily and by the time he reached their old camp the trail left by Rod and Mukoki was already partly obliterated, showing that they had secured an early start up the river.

Bowing his head in the white clouds falling silently about him, Wabi started in swift pursuit. He could not see ten rods ahead of him, so dense was the storm, and at times one side or the other of the river was lost to view. Conditions could not have been better for their flight out of the Woonga country, thought the young hunter. By nightfall they would be many miles up the river, and no sign would be left behind to reveal their former presence or to show in which direction they had gone. For two hours he followed tirelessly over the trail, which became more and more distinct as he proceeded, showing that he was rapidly gaining on his comrades. But even now, though the trail was fresher and deeper, so disguised had it become by falling snow that a passing hunter might have thought a moose or caribou had passed that way.

At the end of the third hour, by which time he figured that he had made at least ten miles, Wabi sat down to rest, and to refresh himself with the lunch which he had taken from the camp that morning. He was surprised at Rod's endurance. That Mukoki and the white boy were still three or four miles ahead of him he did not doubt, unless they, too, had stopped for dinner. This, on further thought, he believed was highly probable. The wilderness about him was intensely still. Not even the twitter of a snow-bird marred its silence. For a long time Wabi sat as immovable as the log upon which he had seated himself, resting and listening. Such a day as this held a peculiar and unusual fascination for him. It was as if the whole world was shut out, and that even the wild things of the forest dared not go abroad in this supreme moment of Nature's handiwork, when with lavish hand she spread the white mantle that was to stretch from the border to Hudson Bay.

As he listened there came to him suddenly a sound that forced from between his lips a half-articulate cry. It was the clear, ringing report of a rifle! And following it there came another, and another, until in quick succession he had counted five!

What did it mean? He sprang to his feet, his heart thumping, every nerve in him prepared for action. He would have sworn it was Mukoki's rifle--yet Mukoki would not have fired at game! They had agreed upon that.

Had Rod and the old Indian been attacked? In another instant Wabi was bounding over the trail with the speed of a deer.

CHAPTER V
MYSTERIOUS SHOTS IN THE WILDERNESS

As the Indian youth sped over the trail in the direction of the rifle-shots he flung his usual caution to the winds. His blood thrilled with the knowledge that there was not a moment to lose--that even now, in all probability, he would be too late to assist his friends. This fear was emphasized by the absolute silence which followed the five shots. Eagerly, almost prayerfully, he listened as he ran for other sounds of battle--for the report of Mukoki's revolver, or the whoops of the victors. If there had been an ambush it was all over now. Each moment added to his conviction, and as he thrust the muzzle of his gun ahead of him, his finger hovering near the trigger and his snow-blinded eyes staring ahead into the storm, something like a sob escaped his lips.

Ahead of him the stream narrowed until it almost buried itself under a mass of towering cedars. The closeness of the forest walls now added to the general gloom, intensified by the first gray pallor of the Northern dusk, which begins to fall in these regions early in the afternoon of November days. For a moment, just before plunging into the gloomy trail between the cedars, Wabi stopped and listened. He heard nothing but the beating of his own heart, which worked like a trip-hammer within his breast. The stillness was oppressive. And the longer he listened the more some invisible power seemed to hold him back. It was not fear, it was not lack of courage, but--

What was there just beyond those cedars, lurking cautiously in the snow gloom?

With instinct that was almost animal in its unreasonableness Wabi sank upon his knees. He had seen nothing, he had heard nothing; but he crouched close, until he was no larger than a waiting wolf, and there was a deadly earnestness in the manner in which he turned his rifle into the deeper gloom of those close-knit walls of forest. Something was approaching, cautiously, stealthily, and with extreme slowness. The Indian boy felt that this was so, and yet if his life had depended upon it he could not have told why. He huddled himself lower in the snow. His eyes gleamed with excitement. Minute after minute passed, and still there came no sound. Then, from far up that dusky avenue of cedars, there came the sudden startled chatter of a moose-bird. It was a warning which years of experience had taught Wabi always to respect. Perhaps a roving fox had frightened it, perhaps the bird had taken to noisy flight at the near tread of a moose, a caribou, or a deer. But--

To Wabi the soft, quick notes of the moose-bird spelled man! In an instant he was upon his feet, darting quickly into the sheltering cedars of the shore. Through these he now made his way with extreme caution, keeping close to the bank of the frozen stream. After a little he paused again and concealed himself behind the end of a fallen log. Ahead of him he could look into the snow gloom between the cedars, and whatever was coming through that gloom would have to pass within a dozen yards of him. Each moment added to his excitement. He heard the chatter of a red squirrel, much nearer than the moose-bird. Once he fancied that he heard the striking of two objects, as though a rifle barrel had accidentally come into contact with the dead limb of a tree.

Suddenly the Indian youth imagined that he saw something--an indistinct shadow that came in the snow gloom, then disappeared, and came again. He brushed the water and snow from his eyes with one of his mittened hands and stared hard and steadily. Once more the shadow disappeared, then came again, larger and more distinct than before. There was no doubt now. Whatever had startled the moose-bird was coming slowly, noiselessly.

Wabi brought his rifle to his shoulder. Life and death hovered with his anxious, naked finger over the gun trigger. But he was too well trained in the ways of the wilderness to fire just yet. Yard by yard the shadow approached, and divided itself into two shadows. Wabi could now see that they were men. They were advancing in a cautious, crouching attitude, as though they expected to meet enemies somewhere ahead of them. Wabi's heart thumped with joy. There could be no surer sign that Mukoki and Rod were still among the living, for why should the Woongas employ this caution if they had already successfully ambushed the hunters? With the chill of a cold hand at his throat the answer flashed into Wabigoon's brain. His friends had been ambushed, and these two Woongas were stealing back over the trail to slay him!

Very slowly, very gently, the young Indian's finger pressed against the trigger of his rifle. A dozen feet more, and then--

The shadows had stopped, and now drew together as if in consultation. They were not more than twenty yards away, and for a moment Wabi lowered his rifle and listened hard. He could hear the low unintelligible mutterings of their conversation. Then there came to him a single incautious reply from one of the shadows.

"All right!"

Surely that was not the English of a Woonga! It sounded like--

In a flash Wabi had called softly.

"Ho, Muky--Muky--Rod!"

In another moment the three wolf hunters were together, silently wringing one another's hands, the death-like pallor of Rod's face and the tense lines in the bronzed countenances of Mukoki and Wabigoon plainly showing the tremendous strain they had been under.

"You shoot?" whispered Mukoki.

"No!" replied Wabi, his eyes widening in surprise. "Didn't *you* shoot?"

"No!"

Only the one word fell from the old Indian, but it was filled with a new warning. Who had fired the five shots? The hunters gazed blankly at one another, mute questioning in their eyes. Without speaking, Mukoki pointed suggestively to the clearer channel of the river beyond the cedars. Evidently he thought the shots had come from there. Wabi shook his head.

"There was no trail," he whispered. "Nobody has crossed the river."

"I thought they were there!" breathed Rod. He pointed into the forest. "But Mukoki said no."

For a long time the three stood and listened. Half a mile back in the forest they heard the howl of a single wolf, and Wabi flashed a curious glance into the eyes of the old Indian.

"That's a man's cry," he whispered. "The wolf has struck a human trail. It isn't mine!"

"Nor ours," replied Rod.

This one long howl of the wolf was the only sound that broke the stillness of approaching night. Mukoki turned, and the others followed in his trail. A quarter of a mile farther on the stream became still narrower and plunged between great masses of rock which rose into wild and precipitous hills that were almost mountains a little way back. No longer could the hunters now follow the channel of the rushing torrent. Through a break in a gigantic wall of rock and huge boulders led the trail of Rod and Mukoki. Ten minutes more and the three had clambered to the top of the ridge where, in the lee of a great rock, the remains of a fire were still burning. Here the old Indian and his companion had struck camp and were waiting for Wabigoon when they heard the shots which they, too, believed were those of an ambush.

A comfortable shelter of balsam had already been erected against the rock, and close beside the fire, where Mukoki had dropped it at the sound of the shots, was a large piece of spitted venison. The situation was ideal for a camp and after the hard day's tramp through the snow the young wolf hunters regarded it with expressions of pleasure, in spite of the enemies whom they knew might be lurking near them. Both Wabi and Rod had accepted the place as their night's home, and were stirring up the fire, when their attention was drawn to the singular attitude of Mukoki. The old warrior stood leaning on his rifle, speechless and motionless, his eyes regarding the process of rekindling the fire with mute disapprobation. Wabi, poised on one knee, looked at him questioningly.

"No make more fire," said the old Indian, shaking his head. "No dare stay here. Go on--beyond mountain!"

Mukoki straightened himself and stretched a long arm toward the north.

"River go like much devil 'long edge of mountain," he continued. "Make heap noise through rock, then make swamp thick for cow moose--then run through mountain and make wide, smooth river once more. We go over mountain. Snow all night. Morning come--no trail for Woonga. We stay here--make big trail in morning. Woonga follow like devil, ver' plain to see!"

Wabi rose to his feet, his face showing the keenness of his disappointment. Since early morning he had been traveling, even running at times, and he was tired enough to risk willingly a few dangers for the sake of sleep and supper. Rod was in even worse condition, though his trail had been much shorter. For a few moments the two boys looked at each other in silence, neither attempting to conceal the lack of favor with which Mukoki's suggestion was received. But Wabi was too wise openly to oppose the old pathfinder. If Mukoki said that it was dangerous for them to remain where they were during the night--well, it was dangerous, and it would be foolish of him to dispute it. He knew Mukoki to be the greatest hunter of his tribe, a human bloodhound on the trail, and what he said was law. So with a cheerful grin at Rod, who needed all the encouragement that could be given to him, Wabi began the readjustment of the pack which he had flung from his shoulders a few minutes before.

"Mountain not ver' far. Two--t'ree mile, then camp," encouraged Mukoki. "Walk slow--have big supper."

Only a few articles had been taken from the toboggan-sled on which the hunters were dragging the greater part of their equipment into the wilderness, and Mukoki soon had these packed again. The three adventurers now took up the new trail along the top of one of those wild and picturesque ridges which both the Indians and white hunters of this great Northland call mountains. Wabigoon led, weighted under his pack, selecting the clearest road for the toboggan and clipping down obstructing saplings with his keen-edged belt-ax. A dozen feet behind him followed Mukoki, dragging the sled; and behind the sled, securely tied with a thong of babeesh, or moose-skin rope, slunk the wolf. Rod, less experienced in making a trail and burdened with a lighter pack, formed the rear of the little cavalcade.

Darkness was now falling rapidly. Though Wabigoon was not more than a dozen yards ahead, Rod could only now and then catch a fleeting vision of him through the gloom. Mukoki, doubled over in his harness, was hardly more than a blotch in the early night. Only the wolf was near enough to offer companionship to the tired and down-spirited youth. Rod's enthusiasm was not easily cooled, but just now he mentally wished that, for this one night at least, he was back at the Post, with the lovely little Minnetaki relating to him some legend of bird or beast they had encountered that day. How much pleasanter that would be! The vision of the bewitching little maiden was suddenly knocked out of his head in a most unexpected and startling way. Mukoki had paused for a moment and Rod, unconscious of the fact, continued on his journey until he tumbled in a sprawling heap over the sled, knocking Mukoki's legs completely from under him in his fall. When Wabi ran back he found Rod flattened out, face downward, and Mukoki entangled in his site harness on top of him.

In a way this accident was fortunate. Wabi, who possessed a Caucasian sense of humor, shook with merriment as he gave his assistance, and Rod, after he had dug the snow from his eyes and ears and had emptied a handful of it from his neck, joined with him.

The ridge now became narrower as the trio advanced. On one side, far down, could be heard the thunderous rush of the river, and from the direction of the sound Rod knew they were near a precipice. Great beds of boulders and broken rock, thrown there by some tumultuous upheaval of past ages, now impeded their progress, and every step was taken with extreme caution. The noise of the torrent became louder and louder as they advanced and on one side of him Rod now thought that he could distinguish a dim massive shadow towering above them, like the precipitous side of a mountain. A few steps farther and Mukoki exchanged places with Wabigoon.

"Muky has been here before," cried Wabi close up to Rod's ear. His voice was almost drowned by the tumult below. "That's where the river rushes through the mountain!"

Rod forgot his fatigue in the new excitement. Never in his wildest dreams of adventure had he foreseen an hour like this. Each step seemed to bring them nearer the edge of the vast chasm through which the river plunged, and yet not a sign of it could he see. He strained his eyes and ears, each moment expecting to hear the warning voice of the old warrior. With a suddenness that chilled him he saw the great shadow close in upon them from the opposite side, and for the first time he realized their position. On their left was the precipice--on their right the sheer wall of the mountain! How wide was the ledge along which they were traveling? His foot struck a stick under the snow. Catching it up he flung it out into space. For a single instant he paused to listen, but there came no sound of the falling object. The precipice was very near--a little chill ran up his spine. It was a sensation he had never experienced in walking the streets of a city!

Though he could not see, he knew that the ledge was now leading them up. He could hear Wabigoon straining ahead of the toboggan and he began to assist by pushing on the rear of the loaded sled. For half an hour this upward climb continued, until the sound of the river had entirely died away. No longer was the mountain on the right. Five minutes later Mukoki called a halt.

"On top mountain," he said briefly. "Camp here!"

Rod could not repress an exclamation of joy, and Wabigoon, as he threw off his harness, gave a suppressed whoop. Mukoki, who seemed tireless, began an immediate search for a site for their camp and after a short breathing-spell Rod and Wabi joined him. The spot chosen was in the shelter of a huge rock, and while Mukoki cleaned away the snow the young hunters set to work with their axes in a near growth of balsam, cutting armful after armful of the soft odorous boughs. Inside of an hour a comfortable camp was completed, with an exhilarating fire throwing its crackling flames high up into the night before it.

For the first time since leaving the abandoned camp at the other end of the ridge the hunters fully realized how famished they were, and Mukoki was at once delegated to prepare supper while Wabi and Rod searched in the darkness for their night's supply of wood. Fortunately quite near at hand they discovered several dead poplars, the best fuel in the world for a camp-fire, and by the time the venison and coffee were ready they had collected a huge pile of this, together with several good-sized backlogs.

Mukoki had spread the feast in the opening of the shelter where the heat of the fire, reflected from the face of the rock, fell upon them in genial warmth, suffusing their faces with a most comfortable glow. The heat, together with the feast, were almost overpowering in their effects, and hardly was his supper completed when Rod felt creeping over him a drowsiness which he attempted in vain to fight off a little longer. Dragging himself back in the shelter he wrapped himself in his blanket, burrowed into the mass of balsam boughs, and passed quickly into oblivion. His last intelligible vision was Mukoki piling logs upon the fire, while the flames shot up a dozen feet into the air, illumining to his drowsy eyes for an instant a wild chaos of rock, beyond which lay the mysterious and impenetrable blackness of the wilderness.

CHAPTER VI
MUKOKI DISTURBS THE ANCIENT SKELETONS

Completely exhausted, every muscle in his aching body still seeming to strain with exertion, the night was one of restless and uncomfortable dreams for Roderick Drew. While Wabi and the old Indian, veterans in wilderness hardship, slept in peace and tranquillity, the city boy found himself in the most unusual and thrilling situations from which he would extricate himself with a grunt or sharp cry, several times sitting bolt upright in his bed of balsam until he realized where he was, and that his adventures were only those of dreamland.

From one of these dreams Rod had aroused himself into drowsy wakefulness. He fancied that he had heard steps. For the tenth time he raised himself upon an elbow, stretched, rubbed his eyes, glanced at the dark, inanimate forms of his sleeping companions, and snuggled down into his balsam boughs again. A few moments later he sat bolt upright. He could have sworn that he heard real steps this time--a soft cautious crunching in the snow very near his head. Breathlessly he listened. Not a sound broke the silence except the snapping of a dying ember in the fire. Another dream! Once more he settled back, drawing his blanket closely about him. Then, for a full breath, the very beating of his heart seemed to cease.

What was that!

He was awake now, wide awake, with every faculty in him striving to arrange itself. He had heard--a step! Slowly, very cautiously this time, he raised himself. There came distinctly to his ears a light crunching in the snow. It seemed back of the shelter--then was moving away, then stopped. The flickering light of the dying fire still played on the face of the great rock. Suddenly, at the very end of that rock, something moved.

Some object was creeping cautiously upon the sleeping camp!

For a moment his thrilling discovery froze the young hunter into inaction. But in a moment the whole situation flashed upon him. The Woongas had followed them! They were about to fall upon the helpless camp! Unexpectedly one of his hands came in contact with the barrel of Wabi's rifle. The touch of the cold steel aroused him. There was no time to awaken his companions. Even as he drew the gun to him he saw the object grow larger and larger at the end of the rock, until it stood crouching, as if about to spring.

One bated breath--a thunderous report--a snarling scream of pain, and the camp was awake!

"We're attacked!" cried Rod. "Quick--Wabi--Mukoki!"

The white boy was on his knees now, the smoking rifle still leveled toward the rocks. Out there, in the thick shadows beyond the fire, a body was groveling and kicking in death agonies. In another instant the gaunt form of the old warrior was beside Rod, his rifle at his shoulder, and over their heads reached Wabigoon's arm, the barrel of his heavy revolver glinting in the firelight.

For a full minute they crouched there, breathless, waiting.

"They've gone!" broke Wabi in a tense whisper.

"I got one of them!" replied Rod, his voice trembling with excitement.

Mukoki slipped back and burrowed a hole through the side of the shelter. He could see nothing. Slowly he slipped out, his rifle ready. The others could hear him as he went. Foot by foot the old warrior slunk along in the deep gloom toward the end of the rock. Now he was almost there, now--

The young hunters saw him suddenly straighten. There came to them a low chuckling grunt. He bent over, seized an object, and flung it in the light of the fire.

"Heap big Woonga! Kill nice fat lynx!"

With a wail, half feigned, half real, Rod flung himself back upon the balsam while Wabi set up a roar that made the night echo. Mukoki's face was creased in a broad grin.

"Heap big Woonga--heem!" he repeated, chuckling. "Nice fat lynx shot well in face. No look like bad man Woonga to Mukoki!"

When Rod finally emerged from his den to join the others his face was flushed and wore what Wabi described as a "sheepish grin."

"It's all right for you fellows to make fun of me," he declared. "But what if they had been Woongas? By George, if we're ever attacked again I won't do a thing. I'll let you fellows fight 'em off!"

In spite of the general merriment at his expense, Rod was immensely proud of his first lynx. It was an enormous creature of its kind, drawn by hunger to the scraps of the camp-fire feast; and it was this animal, as it cautiously inspected the camp, that the young hunter had heard crunching in the snow. Wolf, whose instinct had told him what a mix-up would mean, had slunk into his shelter without betraying his whereabouts to this arch-enemy of his tribe.

With the craft of his race, Mukoki was skinning the animal while it was still warm.

"You go back bed," he said to his companions. "I build big fire again--then sleep."

The excitement of his adventure at least freed Rod from the unpleasantness of further dreams, and it was late the following morning before he awoke again. He was astonished to find that a beautiful sun was shining. Wabi and the old Indian were already outside preparing breakfast, and the cheerful whistling of the former assured Rod that there was now little to be feared from the Woongas. Without lingering to take a beauty nap he joined them.

Everywhere about them lay white winter. The rocks, the trees, and the mountain behind them were covered with two feet of snow and upon it the sun shone with dazzling brilliancy. But it was not until Rod looked into the north that he saw the wilderness in all of its grandeur. The camp had been made at the extreme point of the ridge, and stretching away under his eyes, mile after mile, was the vast white desolation that reached to Hudson Bay. In speechless wonder he gazed down upon the unblazed forests, saw plains and hills unfold themselves as his vision gained distance, followed a river until it was lost in the bewildering picture, and let his eyes rest here and there upon the glistening, snow-smothered bosoms of lakes, rimmed in by walls of black forest. This was not the wilderness as he had expected it to be, nor as he had often read of it in books. It was beautiful! It was magnificent! His heart throbbed with pleasure as he gazed down on it, the blood rose to his face in an excited flush, and he seemed hardly to breathe in his tense interest.

Mukoki had come up beside him softly, and spoke in his low guttural voice.

"Twent' t'ousand moose down there--twent' t'ousand caribou-oo! No man--no house--more twent' t'ousand miles!"

Roderick, even trembling in his new emotion, looked into the old warrior's face. In Mukoki's eyes there was a curious, thrilling gleam. He stared straight out into the unending distance as though his keen vision would penetrate far beyond the last of that visible desolation--on and on, even to the grim and uttermost fastnesses of Hudson Bay. Wabi came up and placed his hand on Rod's shoulder.

"Muky was born off there," he said. "Away beyond where we can see. Those were his hunting-grounds when a boy. See that mountain yonder? You might take it for a cloud. It's thirty miles from here! And that lake down there--you might think a rifle-shot would reach it--is five miles away! If a moose or a caribou or a wolf should cross it how you could see him."

For a few moments longer the three stood silent, then Wabi and the old Indian returned to the fire to finish the preparation of breakfast, leaving Rod alone in his enchantment. What unsolved mysteries, what unwritten tragedies, what romance, what treasure of gold that vast North must hold! For a thousand, perhaps a million centuries, it had lain thus undisturbed in the embrace of nature; few white men had broken its solitudes, and the wild things still lived there as they had lived in the winters of ages and ages ago.

The call to breakfast came almost as an unpleasant interruption to Rod. But it did not shock his appetite as it had his romantic fancies, and he performed his part at the morning meal with considerable credit. Wabi and Mukoki had already decided that they would not take up the trail again that day but would remain in their present camp until the following morning. There were several reasons for this delay.

"We can't travel without snow-shoes now," explained Wabi to Rod, "and we've got to take a day off to teach you how to use them. Then, all the wild things are lying low. Moose, deer, caribou, and especially wolves and fur animals, won't begin traveling much until this afternoon and to-night, and if we took up the trail now we would have no way of telling what kind of a game country we were in. And that is the important thing just now. If we strike a first-rate game country during the next couple days we'll stop and build our winter camp."

"Then you believe we are far enough away from the Woongas?" asked Rod. Mukoki grunted.

"No believe Woongas come over mountain. Heap good game country back there. They stay."

During the meal the white boy asked a hundred questions about the vast wilderness which lay stretched out before them in a great panorama, and in which they were soon to bury themselves, and every answer added to his enthusiasm. Immediately after they had finished eating Rod expressed a desire to begin his study in snow-shoeing, and for an hour after that Wabi and Mukoki piloted him back and forth along the ridge, instructing him in this and in that, applauding when he made an especially good dash and enjoying themselves immensely when he took one of his frequent tumbles into the snow. By noon Rod secretly believed that he was becoming quite an adept.

Although the day in camp was an exceedingly pleasant one for Rod, he could not but observe that at times something seemed to be troubling Wabi. Twice he discovered the Indian youth alone within the shelter sitting in silent and morose dejection, and finally he insisted upon an explanation.

"I want you to tell me what the trouble is, Wabi," he demanded. "What has gone wrong?"

Wabi jumped to his feet with a little laugh.

"Did you ever have a dream that bothered you, Rod?" he asked. "Well, I had one last night, and since then--somehow--I can't keep from worrying about the people back at the Post, and especially about Minnetaki. It's all--what do you call it--bosh? Listen! Wasn't that Mukoki's whistle?"

As he paused Mukoki came running around the end of the rock.

"See fun!" he cried softly. "Quick--see heem quick!"

He turned and darted toward the precipitous edge of the ridge, closely followed by the two boys.

"Cari-boo-oo!" he whispered excitedly as they came up beside him. "Cari-boo-oo--making big play!"

He pointed down into the snowy wilderness. Three-quarters of a mile away, though to Rod apparently not more than a third of that distance from where they stood, half a dozen animals were disporting themselves in a singular fashion in a meadow-like opening between the mountain and a range of forest. It was Rod's first real glimpse of that wonderful animal of the North of which he had read so much, the caribou--commonly known beyond the Sixtieth Degree as the reindeer; and at this moment those below him were indulging in the queer play known in the Hudson Bay regions as the "caribou dance."

"What's the matter with them?" he asked, his voice quivering with excitement. "What--"

"Making big fun!" chuckled Mukoki, drawing the boy closer to the rock that concealed them.

Wabi had thrust a finger in his mouth and now held it above his head, the Indian's truest guide for discovering the direction of the wind. The lee side of his finger remained cold and damp, while that side upon which the breeze fell was quickly dried.

"The wind is toward us, Muky," he announced. "There's a fine chance for a shot. You go! Rod and I will stay here and watch you."

Roderick heard--knew that Mukoki was creeping back to the camp for his rifle, but not for an instant did his spellbound eyes leave the spectacle below him. Two other animals had joined those in the open. He could see the sun glistening on their long antlers as they tossed their heads in their amazing antics. Now three or four of them would dash away with the speed of the wind, as though the deadliest of enemies were close behind them. Two or three hundred yards away they would stop with equal suddenness, whirl about in a circle, as though flight were interrupted on all sides of them, then tear back with lightning speed to rejoin the herd. In twos and threes and fours they performed these evolutions again and again. But there was another antic that held Rod's eyes, and if it had not been so new and wonderful to him he would have laughed, as Wabi was doing--silently--behind him. From out of the herd would suddenly dash one of the agile creatures, whirl about, jump and kick, and finally bounce up and down on all four feet, as though performing a comedy sketch in pantomime for the amusement of its companions; and when this was done it would start out in another mad flight, with others of the herd at its heels.

"They are the funniest, swiftest, and shrewdest animals in the North," said Wabi. "They can smell you over a mountain if the wind is right, and hear you for half a mile. Look!"

He pointed downward over Rod's shoulder. Mukoki had already reached the base of the ridge and was stealing straight out in the direction of the caribou. Rod gave a surprised gasp.

"Great Scott! They'll see him, won't they?" he cried.

"Not if Mukoki knows himself," smiled the Indian youth. "Remember that we are looking down on things. Everything seems clear and open to us, while in reality it's quite thick down there. I'll bet Muky can't see one hundred yards ahead of him. He has got his bearings and will go as straight as though he was on a blazed trail; but he won't see the caribou until he conies to the edge of the open."

Each minute now added to Rod's excitement. Each of those minutes brought the old warrior nearer his game. Seldom, thought Rod, had such a scene been unfolded to the eyes of a white boy. The complete picture--the playful rompings of the dumb children of the wilderness; the stealthy approach of the old Indian; every rock, every tree that was to play its part--all were revealed to their eyes. Not a phase in this drama in wild life escaped them. Five minutes, ten, fifteen passed. They could see Mukoki as he stopped and lifted a hand to test the wind. Then he crouched, advancing foot by foot, yard by yard, so slowly that he seemed to be on his hands and knees.

"He can hear them, but he can't see them!" breathed Wabigoon. "See! He places his ear to the ground! Now he has got his bearings again--as straight as a die! Good old Muky!"

The old Indian crept on. In his excitement Rod clenched his hands and he seemed to live without breathing. Would Mukoki never shoot? Would he **never** shoot? He seemed now to be within a stone's throw of the herd.

"How far, Wabi?"

"Four hundred yards, perhaps five," replied the Indian. "It's a long shot! He can't see them yet."

Rod gripped his companion's arm.

Mukoki had stopped. Down and down he slunk, until he became only a blot in the snow.

"Now!"

There came a moment of startled silence. In the midst of their play the animals in the open stood for a single instant paralyzed by a knowledge of impending danger, and in that instant there came to the young hunters the report of Mukoki's rifle.

"No good!" cried Wabi.

In his excitement he leaped to his feet. The caribou had turned and the whole eight of them were racing across the open. Another shot, and another--three in quick succession, and one of the fleeing animals fell, scrambled to its knees--and plunged on again! A fifth shot--the last in Mukoki's rifle! Again the wounded animal fell, struggled to its knees--to its forefeet--and fell again.

"Good work! Five hundred yards if it was a foot!" exclaimed Wabigoon with a relieved laugh. "Fresh steak for supper, Rod!"

Mukoki came out into the open, reloading his rifle. Quickly he moved across the wilderness playground, now crimson with blood, unsheathed his knife, and dropped upon his knees close to the throat of the slain animal.

"I'll go down and give him a little help, Rod," said Wabi. "Your legs are pretty sore, and it's a hard climb down there; so if you will keep up the fire, Mukoki and I will bring back the meat."

During the next hour Rod busied himself with collecting firewood for the night and in practising with his snow-shoes. He was astonished to find how swiftly and easily he could travel in them, and was satisfied that he could make twenty miles a day even as a tenderfoot.

Left to his own thoughts he found his mind recurring once more to the Woongas and Minnetaki. Why was Wabi worried? Inwardly he did not believe that it was a dream alone that was troubling him. There was still some cause for fear. Of that he was certain. And why would not the Woongas penetrate beyond this mountain? He had asked himself this question a score of times during the last twenty-four hours, in spite of the fact that both Mukoki and Wabigoon were quite satisfied that they were well out of the Woonga territory.

It was growing dusk when Wabi and the old Indian returned with the meat of the caribou. No time was lost in preparing supper, for the hunters had decided that the next day's trail would begin with dawn and probably end with darkness, which meant that they would require all the rest they could get before then. They were all eager to begin the winter's hunt. That day Mukoki's eyes had glistened at each fresh track he encountered. Wabi and Rod were filled with enthusiasm. Even Wolf, now and then stretching his gaunt self, would nose the air with eager suspicion, as if longing for the excitement of the tragedies in which he was to play such an important part.

"If you can stand it," said Wabi, nodding at Rod over his caribou steak, "we won't lose a minute from now on. Over that country we ought to make twenty-five or thirty miles to-morrow. We may strike our hunting-ground by noon, or it may take us two or three days; but in either event we haven't any time to waste. Hurrah for the big camp, I say--and our fun begins!"

It seemed to Rod as though he had hardly fallen asleep that night when somebody began tumbling him about in his bed of balsam. Opening his eyes he beheld Wabi's laughing face, illuminated in the glow of a roaring fire.

"Time's up!" he called cheerily. "Hustle out, Rod. Breakfast is sizzling hot, everything is packed, and here you are still dreaming of--what?"

"Minnetaki!" shot back Rod with unblushing honesty.

In another minute he was outside, straightening his disheveled garments and smoothing his tousled hair. It was still very dark, but Rod assured himself by his watch that it was nearly four o'clock. Mukoki had already placed their breakfast on a flat rock beside the fire and, according to Wabigoon's previous scheme, no time was lost in disposing of it.

Dawn was just breaking when the little cavalcade of adventurers set out from the camp. More keenly than ever Rod now felt the loss of his rifle. They were about to enter upon a hunter's paradise--and he had no gun! His disappointment was acute and he could not repress a confession of his feelings to Wabi. The Indian youth at once suggested a happy remedy. They would take turns in using his gun, Rod to have it one day and he the next; and Wabi's heavy revolver would also change hands, so that the one who did not possess the rifle would be armed with the smaller weapon. This solution of the difficulty lifted a dampening burden from Rod's heart, and when the little party began its descent into the wilderness regions under the mountain the city lad carried the rifle, for Wabi insisted that he have the first "turn."

Once free of the rock-strewn ridge the two boys joined forces in pulling the toboggan while Mukoki struck out a trail ahead of them. As it became lighter Rod found his eyes glued with keen interest to Mukoki's snow-shoes, and for the first time in his life he realized what it really meant to "make a trail." The old Indian was the most famous trailmaker as well as the keenest trailer of his tribe, and in the comparatively open bottoms through which they were now traveling he was in his element. His strides were enormous, and with each stride he threw up showers of snow, leaving a broad level path behind him in which the snow was packed by his own weight, so that when Wabi and Rod came to follow him they were not impeded by sinking into a soft surface.

Half a mile from the mountain Mukoki stopped and waited for the others to come up to him.

"Moose!" he called, pointing at a curious track in the snow.

Rod leaned eagerly over the track.

"The snow is still crumbling and falling where he stepped," said Wabi. "Watch that little chunk, Rod. See--it's slipping--down--down--there! It was an old bull--a big fellow--and he passed here less than an hour ago."

Signs of the night carnival of the wild things now became more and more frequent as the hunters advanced. They crossed and recrossed the trail of a fox; and farther on they discovered where this little pirate of darkness had slaughtered a big white rabbit. The snow was covered with blood and hair and part of the carcass remained uneaten. Again Wabi forgot his determination to waste no time and paused to investigate.

"Now, if we only knew what kind of a fox he was!" he exclaimed to Rod. "But we don't. All we know is that he's a fox. And all fox tracks are alike, no matter what kind of a fox makes them. If there was only some difference our fortunes would be made!"

"How?" asked Rod.

Mukoki chuckled as if the mere thought of such a possibility filled him with glee.

"Well, that fellow may be an ordinary red fox," explained the Indian youth. "If so, he is only worth from ten to twenty dollars; or he may be a black fox, worth fifty or sixty; or what we call a 'cross'--a mixture of silver and black--worth from seventy-five to a hundred. Or--"

"Heap big silver!" interrupted Mukoki with another chuckle.

"Yes, or a silver," finished Wabi. "A poor silver is worth two hundred dollars, and a good one from five hundred to a thousand! Now do you see why we would like to have a difference in the tracks? If that was a silver, a black or a 'cross,' we'd follow him; but in all probability he is red."

Every hour added to Rod's knowledge of the wilderness and its people. For the first time in his life he saw the big dog-like tracks made by wolves, the dainty hoofprints of the red deer and the spreading imprints of a traveling lynx; he pictured the hugeness of the moose that made a track as big as his head, discovered how to tell the difference between the hoof-print of a small moose and a big caribou, and in almost every mile learned something new.

Half a dozen times during the morning the hunters stopped to rest. By noon Wabi figured that they had traveled twenty miles, and, although very tired, Rod declared that he was still "game for another ten." After dinner the aspect of the country changed. The river which they had been following became narrower and was so swift in places that it rushed tumultuously between its frozen edges. Forest-clad hills, huge boulders and masses of rock now began to mingle again with the bottoms, which in this country are known as plains. Every mile added to the roughness and picturesque grandeur of the country. A few miles to the east rose another range of wild and rugged hills; small lakes became more and more numerous, and everywhere the hunters crossed and recrossed frozen creeks.

And each step they took now added to the enthusiasm of Wabi and his companions. Evidences of game and fur animals were plenty. A thousand ideal locations for a winter camp were about them, and their progress became slow and studied.

A gently sloping hill of considerable height now lay in their path and Mukoki led the ascent. At the top the three paused in joyful astonishment. At their feet lay a "dip," or hollow, a dozen acres in extent, and in the center of this dip was a tiny lake partly surrounded by a mixed forest of cedar, balsam and birch that swept back over the hill, and partly inclosed by a meadow-like opening. One might have traveled through the country a thousand times without discovering this bit of wilderness paradise hidden in a hilltop. Without speaking Mukoki threw off his heavy pack. Wabi unbuckled his harness and relieved his shoulders of their burden. Rod, following their example, dropped his small pack beside that of the old Indian, and Wolf, straining at his babeesh thong, gazed with eager eyes into the hollow as though he, too, knew that it was to be their winter home.

Wabi broke the silence.

"How is that, Muky?" he asked.

Mukoki chuckled with unbounded satisfaction.

"Ver' fine. No get bad wind--never see smoke--plenty wood--plenty water."

Relieved of their burdens, and leaving Wolf tied to the toboggan, the hunters made their way down to the lake. Hardly had they reached its edge when Wabi halted with a startled exclamation and pointed into the forest on the opposite side.

"Look at that!"

A hundred yards away, almost concealed among the trees, was a cabin. Even from where they stood they could see that it was deserted. Snow was drifted high about it. No chimney surmounted its roof. Nowhere was there a sign of life.

Slowly the hunters approached. It was evident that the cabin was very old. The logs of which it was built were beginning to decay. A mass of saplings had taken root upon its roof, and everything about it gave evidence that it had been erected many years before. The door, made of split timber and opening toward the lake, was closed; the one window, also opening upon the lake, was tightly barred with lengths of sapling.

Mukoki tried the door, but it resisted his efforts. Evidently it was strongly barred from within.

Curiosity now gave place to astonishment.

How could the door be locked within, and the window barred from within, without there being somebody inside?

For a few moments the three stood speechless, listening.

"Looks queer, doesn't it?" spoke Wabi softly.

Mukoki had dropped on his knees beside the door. He could hear no sound. Then he kicked off his snow-shoes, gripped his belt-ax and stepped to the window.

A dozen blows and one of the bars fell. The old Indian sniffed suspiciously, his ear close to the opening. Damp, stifling air greeted his nostrils, but still there was no sound. One after another he knocked off the remaining bars and thrust his head and shoulders inside. Gradually his eyes became accustomed to the darkness and he pulled himself in.

Half-way--and he stopped.

"Go on, Muky," urged Wabi, who was pressing close behind.

There came no answer from the old Indian. For a full minute he remained poised there, as motionless as a stone, as silent as death.

Then, very slowly--inch by inch, as though afraid of awakening a sleeping person, he lowered himself to the ground. When he turned toward the young hunters it was with an expression that Rod had never seen upon Mukoki's face before.

"What is it, Mukoki?"

The old Indian gasped, as if for fresh air.

"Cabin--she filled with twent' t'ousand dead men!" he replied.

CHAPTER VII
RODERICK DISCOVERS THE BUCKSKIN BAG

For one long breath Rod and Wabi stared at their companion, only half believing, yet startled by the strange look in the old warrior's face.

"Twent' t'ousand dead men!" he repeated. As he raised his hand, partly to give emphasis and partly to brush the cobwebs from his face, the boys saw it trembling in a way that even Wabi had never witnessed before.

"Ugh!"

In another instant Wabi was at the window, head and shoulders in, as Mukoki had been before him. After a little he pulled himself back and as he glanced at Rod he laughed in an odd thrilling way, as though he had been startled, but not so much so as Mukoki, who had prepared him for the sight which had struck his own vision with the unexpectedness of a shot in the back.

"Take a look, Rod!"

With his breath coming in little uneasy jerks Rod approached the black aperture. A queer sensation seized upon him--a palpitation, not of fear, but of something; a very unpleasant feeling that seemed to choke his breath, and made him wish that he had not been asked to peer into that mysterious darkness. Slowly he thrust his head through the hole. It was as black as night inside. But gradually the darkness seemed to be dispelled. He saw, in a little while, the opposite wall of the cabin. A table outlined itself in deep shadows, and near the table there was a pile of something that he could not name; and tumbled over that was a chair, with an object that might have been an old rag half covering it.

His eyes traveled nearer. Outside Wabi and Mukoki heard a startled, partly suppressed cry. The boy's hands gripped the sides of the window. Fascinated, he stared down upon an object almost within arm's reach of him.

There, leaning against the cabin wall, was what half a century or more ago had been a living man! Now it was a mere skeleton, a grotesque, terrible-looking object, its empty eye-sockets gleaming dully with the light from the window, its grinning mouth, distorted into ghostly life by the pallid mixture of light and gloom, turned full up at him!

Rod fell back, trembling and white.

"I only saw one," he gasped, remembering Mukoki's excited estimate.

Wabi, who had regained his composure, laughed as he struck him two or three playful blows on the back. Mukoki only grunted.

"You didn't look long enough, Rod!" he cried banteringly. "He got on your nerves too quick. I don't blame you, though. By George, I'll bet the shivers went up Muky's back when he first saw 'em! I'm going in to open the door."

Without trepidation the young Indian crawled through the window. Rod, whose nervousness was quickly dispelled, made haste to follow him, while Mukoki again threw his weight against the door. A few blows of Wabi's belt-ax and the door shot inward so suddenly that the old Indian went sprawling after it upon all fours.

A flood of light filled the interior of the cabin. Instinctively Rod's eyes sought the skeleton against the wall. It was leaning as if, many years before, a man had died there in a posture of sleep. Quite near this ghastly tenant of the cabin, stretched at full length upon the log floor, was a second skeleton, and near the overturned chair was a small cluttered heap of bones which were evidently those of some animal. Rod and Wabi drew nearer the skeleton against the wall and were bent upon making a closer examination when an exclamation from Mukoki attracted their attention to the old pathfinder. He was upon his knees beside the second skeleton, and as the boys approached he lifted eyes to them that were filled with unbounded amazement, at the same time pointing a long forefinger to come object among the bones.

"Knife--fight--heem killed!"

Plunged to the hilt in what had once been the breast of a living being, the boys saw a long, heavy-bladed knife, its handle rotting with age, its edges eaten by rust--but still erect, held there by the murderous road its owner had cleft for it through the flesh and bone of his victim.

Rod, who had fallen upon his knees, gazed up blankly; his jaw dropped, and he asked the first question that popped into his head.

"Who--did it?"

Mukoki chuckled, almost gleefully, and nodded toward the gruesome thing reclining against the wall.

"Heem!"

Moved by a common instinct the three drew near the other skeleton. One of its long arms was resting across what had once been a pail, but which, long since, had sunk into total collapse between its hoops. The finger-bones of this arm were still tightly shut, clutching between them a roll of something that looked like birchbark. The remaining arm had fallen close to the skeleton's side, and it was on this side that Mukoki's critical eyes searched most carefully, his curiosity being almost immediately satisfied by the discovery of a short, slant-wise cut in one of the ribs.

"This un die here!" he explained. "Git um stuck knife in ribs. Bad way die! Much hurt--no die quick, sometime. Ver' bad way git stuck!"

"Ugh!" shuddered Rod. "This cabin hasn't had any fresh air in it for a century, I'll bet. Let's get out!"

Mukoki, in passing, picked up a skull from the heap of bones near the chair.

"Dog!" he grunted. "Door lock'--window shut--men fight--both kill. Dog starve!"

As the three retraced their steps to the spot where Wolf was guarding the toboggan, Rod's imaginative mind quickly painted a picture of the terrible tragedy that had occurred long ago in the old cabin. To Mukoki and Wabigoon the discovery of the skeletons was simply an incident in a long life of wilderness adventure--something of passing interest, but of small importance. To Rod it was the most tragic event that had ever come into his city-bound existence, with the exception of the thrilling conflict at Wabinosh House. He reconstructed that deadly hour in the cabin; saw the men in fierce altercation, saw them struggling, and almost heard the fatal blows as they were struck--the blows that slew one with the suddenness of a lightning bolt and sent the other, triumphant but dying, to breathe his last moments with his back propped against the wall. And the dog! What part had he taken? And after that--long days of maddening loneliness, days of starvation and of thirst, until he, too, doubled himself up on the floor and died. It was a terrible, a thrilling picture that burned in Roderick's brain. But why had they quarreled? What cause had there been for that sanguinary night duel? Instinctively Rod accepted it as having occurred at night, for the door had been locked, the window barred. Just then he would have given a good deal to have had the mystery solved.

At the top of the hill Rod awoke to present realities. Wabi, who had harnessed himself to the toboggan, was in high spirits.

"That cabin is a dandy!" he exclaimed as Rod joined him. "It would have taken us at least two weeks to build as good a one. Isn't it luck?"

"We're going to live in it?" inquired his companion.

"Live in it! I should say we were. It is three times as big as the shack we had planned to build. I can't understand why two men like those fellows should have put up such a large cabin. What do you think, Mukoki?"

Mukoki shook his head. Evidently the mystery of the whole thing, beyond the fact that the tenants of the cabin had killed themselves in battle, was beyond his comprehension.

The winter outfit was soon in a heap beside the cabin door.

"Now for cleaning up," announced Wabi cheerfully. "Muky, you lend me a hand with the bones, will you? Rod can nose around and fetch out anything he likes."

This assignment just suited Rod's curiosity. He was now worked up to a feverish pitch of expectancy. Might he not discover some clue that would lead to a solution of the mystery?

One question alone seemed to ring incessantly in his head. Why had they fought? *Why had they fought?*

He even found himself repeating this under his breath as he began rummaging about. He kicked over the old chair, which was made of saplings nailed together, scrutinized a heap of rubbish that crumbled to dust under his touch, and gave a little cry of exultation when he found two guns leaning in a corner of the cabin. Their stocks were decaying; their locks were encased with rust, their barrels, too, were thick with the accumulated rust of years. Carefully, almost tenderly, he took one of these relics of a past age in his hands. It was of ancient pattern, almost as long as he was tall.

"Hudson Bay gun--the kind they had before my father was born!" said Wabi.

With bated breath and eagerly beating heart Rod pursued his search. On one of the walls he found the remains of what had once been garments--part of a hat, that fell in a thousand pieces when he touched it; the dust-rags of a coat and other things that he could not name. On the table there were rusty pans, a tin pail, an iron kettle, and the remains of old knives, forks and spoons. On one end of this table there was an unusual-looking object, and he touched it. Unlike the other rags it did not crumble, and when he lifted it he found that it was a small bag, made of buckskin, tied at the end--and heavy! With trembling fingers he tore away the rotted string and out upon the table there rattled a handful of greenish-black, pebbly looking objects.

Rod gave a sharp quick cry for the others.

Wabi and Mukoki had just come through the door after bearing out one of their gruesome loads, and the young Indian hurried to his side. He weighed one of the pieces in the palm of his hand.

"It's lead, or--"

"Gold!" breathed Rod.

He could hear his own heart thumping as Wabi jumped back to the light of the door, his sheath-knife in his hand. For an instant the keen blade sank into the age-discolored object, and before Rod could see into the crease that it made Wabi's voice rose in an excited cry.

"It's a gold nugget!"

"And *that's* why they fought!" exclaimed Rod exultantly.

He had hoped--and he had discovered the reason. For a few moments this was of more importance to him than the fact that he had found gold. Wabi and Mukoki were now in a panic of excitement. The buckskin bag was turned inside out; the table was cleared of every other object; every nook and cranny was searched with new enthusiasm. The searchers hardly spoke. Each was intent upon finding--finding--finding. Thus does gold--virgin gold--stir up the sparks of that latent, feverish fire which is in every man's soul. Again Rod joined in the search. Every rag, every pile of dust, every bit of unrecognizable debris was torn, sifted and scattered. At the end of an hour the three paused, hopelessly baffled, even keenly disappointed for the time.

"I guess that's all there is," said Wabi.

It was the longest sentence that he had spoken for half an hour.

"There is only one thing to do, boys. We'll clean out everything there is in the cabin, and to-morrow we'll tear up the floor. You can't tell what there might be under it, and we've got to have a new floor anyway. It is getting dusk, and if we have this place fit to sleep in to-night we have got to hustle."

No time was lost in getting the debris of the cabin outside, and by the time darkness had fallen a mass of balsam boughs had been spread upon the log floor just inside the door, blankets were out, packs and supplies stowed away in one corner, and everything "comfortable and shipshape," as Rod expressed it. A huge fire was built a few feet away from the open door and the light and heat from this made the interior of the cabin quite light and warm, and, with the assistance of a couple of candles, more home-like than any camp they had slept in thus far. Mukoki's supper was a veritable feast--broiled caribou, cold beans that the old Indian had cooked at their last camp, meal cakes and hot coffee. The three happy hunters ate of it as though they had not tasted food for a week.

The day, though a hard one, had been fraught with too much excitement for them to retire to their blankets immediately after this meal, as they had usually done in other camps. They realized, too, that they had reached the end of their journey and that their hardest work was over. There was no long jaunt ahead of them to-morrow. Their new life--the happiest life in the world to them--had already begun. Their camp was established, they were ready for their winter's sport, and from this moment on they felt that their evenings were their own to do with as they pleased.

So for many hours that night Rod, Mukoki and Wabigoon sat up and talked and kept the fire roaring before the door. Twenty times they went over the tragedy of the old cabin; twenty times they weighed the half-pound of precious little lumps in the palms of their hands, and bit by bit they built up that life romance of the days of long ago, when all this wilderness was still an unopened book to the white man. And that story seemed very clear to them now. These men had been prospectors. They had discovered gold. Afterward they had quarreled, probably over some division of it--perhaps over the ownership of the very nuggets they had found; and then, in the heat of their anger, had followed the knife battle.

But where had they discovered the gold? That was the question of supreme interest to the hunters, and they debated it until midnight. There were no mining tools in the camp; no pick, shovel or pan. Then it occurred to them that the builders of the cabin had been hunters, had discovered gold by accident and had collected that in the buckskin bag without the use of a pan.

There was little sleep in the camp that night, and with the first light of day the three were at work again. Immediately after breakfast the task of tearing up the old and decayed floor began. One by one the split saplings were pried up and carried out for firewood, until the earth floor lay bare. Every foot of it was now eagerly turned over with a shovel which had been brought in the equipment; the base-logs were undermined, and filled in again; the moss that had been packed in the chinks between the cabin timbers was dug out, and by noon there was not a square inch of the interior of the camp that had not been searched.

There was no more gold.

In a way this fact brought relief with it. Both Wabi and Rod gradually recovered from their nervous excitement. The thought of gold gradually faded from their minds; the joy and exhilaration of the "hunt life" filled them more and more. Mukoki set to work cutting fresh cedars for the floor; the two boys scoured every log with water from the lake and afterward gathered several bushels of moss for refilling the chinks. That evening supper was cooked on the sheet-iron "section stove" which they had brought on the toboggan, and which was set up where the ancient stove of flat stones had tumbled into ruin. By candle-light the work of "rechinking" with moss progressed rapidly. Wabi was constantly bursting into snatches of wild Indian song, Rod whistled until his throat was sore and Mukoki chuckled and grunted and talked with constantly increasing volubility. A score of times they congratulated one another upon their good luck. Eight wolf-scalps, a fine lynx and nearly two hundred dollars in gold--all within their first week! It was enough to fill them with enthusiasm and they made little effort to repress their joy.

During this evening Mukoki boiled up a large pot of caribou fat and bones, and when Rod asked what kind of soup he was making he responded by picking up a handful of steel traps and dropping them into the mixture.

"Make traps smell good for fox--wolf--fisher, an' marten, too; heem come--all come--like smell," he explained.

"If you don't dip the traps," added Wabi, "nine fur animals out of ten, and wolves most of all, will fight shy of the bait. They can smell the human odor you leave on the steel when you handle it. But the grease 'draws' them."

When the hunters wrapped themselves in their blankets that night their wilderness home was complete. All that remained to be done was the building of three bunks against the ends of the cabin, and this work it was agreed could be accomplished at odd hours by any one who happened to be in camp. In the morning, laden with traps, they would strike out their first hunting-trails, keeping their eyes especially open for signs of wolves; for Mukoki was the greatest wolf hunter in all the Hudson Bay region.

CHAPTER VIII
HOW WOLF BECAME THE COMPANION OF MEN

Twice that night Rod was awakened by Mukoki opening the cabin door. The second time he raised himself upon his elbows and quietly watched the old warrior. It was a brilliantly clear night and a flood of moonlight was pouring into the camp. He could hear Mukoki chuckling and grunting, as though communicating with himself, and at last, his curiosity getting the better of him, he wrapped his blanket about him and joined the Indian at the door.

Mukoki was peering up into space. Rod followed his gaze. The moon was directly above the cabin. The sky was clear of clouds and so bright was the light that objects on the farther side of the lake were plainly visible.

Besides, it was bitter cold--so cold that his face began to tingle as he stood there. These things he noticed, but he could see nothing to hold Mukoki's vision in the sky above unless it was the glorious beauty of the night.

"What is it, Mukoki?" he asked.

The old Indian looked silently at him for a moment, some mysterious, all-absorbing joy revealed in every lineament of his face.

"Wolf night!" he whispered.

He looked back to where Wabi was sleeping.

"Wolf night!" he repeated, and slipped like a shadow to the side of the unconscious young hunter. Rod regarded his actions with growing wonder. He saw him bend over Wabi, shake him by the shoulders, and heard him repeat again, "Wolf night! Wolf night!"

Wabi awoke and sat up in his blankets, and Mukoki came back to the door. He had dressed himself before this, and now, with his rifle, slipped out into the night. The young Indian had joined Rod at the open door and together they watched Mukoki's gaunt figure as it sped swiftly across the lake, up the hill and over into the wilderness desolation beyond.

When Rod looked at Wabi he saw that the Indian boy's eyes were wide and staring, with an expression in them that was something between fright and horror. Without speaking he went to the table and lighted the candles and then dressed. When he was done his face still bore traces of suppressed excitement.

He ran back to the door and whistled loudly. From his shelter beside the cabin the captive wolf responded with a snarling whine. Again he whistled, a dozen times, twenty, but there came no reply. More swiftly than Mukoki the Indian youth sped across the lake and to the summit of the hill. Mukoki had completely disappeared in the white, brilliant vastness of the wilderness that stretched away at his feet.

When Wabi returned to the cabin Rod had a fire roaring in the stove. He seated himself beside it, holding out a pair of hands blue with cold.

"Ugh! It's an awful night!" he shivered.

He laughed across at Rod, a little uneasily, but with the old light back in his eyes. Suddenly he asked:

"Did Minnetaki ever tell you--anything--queer--about Mukoki, Rod?"

"Nothing more than you have told me yourself."

"Well, once in a great while Mukoki has--not exactly a fit, but a little mad spell! I have never determined to my own satisfaction whether he is really out of his head or not. Sometimes I think he is and sometimes I think he is not. But the Indians at the Post believe that at certain times he goes crazy over wolves."

"Wolves!" exclaimed Rod.

"Yes, wolves. And he has good reason. A good many years ago, just about when you and I were born, Mukoki had a wife and child. My mother and others at the Post say that he was especially gone over the kid. He wouldn't hunt like other Indians, but would spend whole days at his shack playing with it and teaching it to do things; and when he did go hunting he would often tote it on his back, even when it wasn't much more than a squalling papoose. He was the happiest Indian at the Post, and one of the poorest. One day Mukoki came to the Post with a little bundle of fur, and most of the things he got in exchange for it, mother says, were for the kid. He reached the store at night and expected to leave for home the next noon, which would bring him to his camp before dark. But something delayed him and he didn't get started until the morning after. Meanwhile, late in the afternoon of the day when he was to have been home, his wife bundled up the kid and they set out to meet him. Well--"

A weird howl from the captive wolf interrupted Wabi for a moment.

"Well, they went on and on, and of course did not meet him. And then, the people at the Post say, the mother must have slipped and hurt herself. Anyway, when Mukoki came over the trail the next day he found them half eaten by wolves. From that day on Mukoki was a different Indian. He became the greatest wolf hunter in all these regions. Soon after the tragedy he came to the Post to live and since then he has not left Minnetaki and me. Once in a great while when the night is just right, when the moon is shining and it is bitter cold, Mukoki seems to go a little mad. He calls this a 'wolf night.' No one can stop him from going out; no one can get him to talk; he will allow no one to accompany him when in such a mood. He will walk miles and miles to-night. But he will come back. And when he returns he will be as sane as you and I, and if you ask him where he has been he will say that he went out to see if he could get a shot at something."

Rod had listened in rapt attention. To him, as Wabi proceeded with his story of the tragedy in Mukoki's life, the old Indian was transformed into another being. No longer was he a mere savage reclaimed a little from the wilderness. There had sprung up in Rod's breast a great, human, throbbing sympathy for him, and in the dim candle-glow his eyes glistened with a dampness which he made no attempt to conceal.

"What does Mukoki mean by 'wolf night'?" he asked.

"Muky is a wizard when it comes to hunting wolves," Wabi went on. "He has studied them and thought of them every day of his life for nearly twenty years. He knows more about wolves than all the rest of the hunters in this country together. He can catch them in every trap he sets, which no other trapper in the world can do; he can tell you a hundred different things about a certain wolf simply by its track, and because of his wonderful knowledge he can tell, by some instinct that is almost supernatural, when a 'wolf night' comes. Something in the air to-night, something in the sky--in the moon--in the very way the wilderness looks, tells him that stray wolves in the plains and hills are 'packing' or banding together to-night, and that in the morning the sun will be shining, and they will be on the sunny sides of the mountains. See if I am not right. To-morrow night, if Mukoki comes back by then, we shall have some exciting sport with the wolves, and then you will see how Wolf out there does his work!"

There followed several minutes of silence. The fire roared up the chimney, the stove glowed red hot and the boys sat and looked and listened. Rod took out his watch. It lacked only ten minutes of midnight. Yet neither seemed possessed with a desire to return to their interrupted sleep.

"Wolf is a curious beast," mused Wabi softly. "You might think he was a sneaking, traitorous cur of a wolf to turn against his own breed and lure them to death. But he isn't. Wolf, as well as Mukoki, has good cause for what he does. You might call it animal vengeance. Did you ever notice that a half of one of his ears is gone? And if you thrust back his head you will find a terrible scar in his throat, and from his left side just back of the fore leg a chunk of flesh half as big as my hand has been torn away. We caught Wolf in a lynx trap, Mukoki and I. He wasn't much more than a whelp then--about six months old, Mukoki said. And while he was in the trap, helpless and unable to defend himself, three or four of his lovely tribe jumped upon him and tried to kill him for breakfast. We hove in sight just in time to drive the cannibals off. We kept Wolf, sewed up his side and throat, tamed him--and to-morrow night you will see how Mukoki has taught him to get even with his people."

It was two hours later when Rod and Wabigoon extinguished the candles and returned to their blankets. And for another hour after that the former found it impossible to sleep. He wondered where Mukoki was--wondered what he was doing, and how in his strange madness he found his way in the trackless wilderness.

When he finally fell asleep it was to dream of the Indian mother and her child; only after a little there was no child, and the woman changed into Minnetaki, and the ravenous wolves into men. From this unpleasant picture he was aroused by a series of prods in his side, and opening his eyes he beheld Wabi in his blankets a yard away, pointing over and beyond him and nodding his head. Rod looked, and caught his breath.

There was Mukoki--peeling potatoes!

"Hello, Muky!" he shouted.

The old Indian looked up with a grin. His face bore no signs of his mad night on the trail. He nodded cheerfully and proceeded with the preparation of breakfast as though he had just risen from his blankets after a long night's rest.

"Better get up," he advised. "Big day's hunt. Much fine sunshine to-day. Find wolves on mountain--plenty wolves!"

The boys tumbled from their blankets and began dressing.

"What time did you get in?" asked Wabi.

"Now," replied Mukoki, pointing to the hot stove and the peeled potatoes. "Just make fire good."

Wabi gave Rod a suggestive look as the old Indian bent over the stove.

"What were you doing last night?" he questioned.

"Big moon--might get shot," grunted Mukoki. "See lynx on hill. See wolf-tracks on red deer trail. No shot."

This was as much of the history of Mukoki's night on the trail as the boys could secure, but during their breakfast Wabi shot another glance at Rod, and as Mukoki left the table for a moment to close the damper in the stove he found an opportunity to whisper:

"See if I'm not right. He will choose the mountain trail." When their companion returned, he said: "We had better split up this morning, hadn't we, Muky? It looks to me as though there are two mighty good lines for traps--one over the hill, where that creek leads off through the range of ridges to the east, and the other along the creek which runs through the hilly plains to the north. What do you think of it?"

"Good" agreed the old hunter. "You two go north--I take ridges."

"No, you and I will take the ridges and Wabi will go north alone," amended Rod quickly. "I'm going with you, Mukoki!"

Mukoki, who was somewhat flattered by this preference of the white youth, grinned and chuckled and began to talk more volubly about the plans which were in his head. It was agreed that they all would return to the cabin at an early hour in the afternoon, for the old Indian seemed positive that they would have their first wolf hunt that night.

Rod noticed that the captive wolf received no breakfast that morning, and he easily guessed the reason.

The traps were now divided. Three different sizes had been brought from the

Post--fifty small ones for mink, marten and other small fur animals; fifteen fox traps, and as many larger ones for lynx and wolves. Wabi equipped himself with twenty of the small traps and four each of fox and lynx traps, while Rod and Mukoki took about forty in all. The remainder of the caribou meat was then cut into chunks and divided equally among them for bait.

The sun was just beginning to show itself above the wilderness when the hunters left camp. As Mukoki had predicted, it was a glorious day, one of those bitterly cold, cloudless days when, as the Indians believe, the great Creator robs the rest of the world of the sun that it may shine in all its glory upon their own savage land. From the top of the hill that sheltered their home Rod looked out over the glistening forests and lakes in rapt and speechless admiration; but only for a few moments did the three pause, then took up their different trails.

At the foot of this hill Mukoki and his companion struck the creek. They had not progressed more than fifty rods when the old Indian stopped and pointed at a fallen log which spanned the stream. The snow on this log was beaten by tiny footprints. Mukoki gazed a moment, cast an observant eye along the trail, and at once threw off his pack.

"Mink!" he explained. He crossed the frozen creek, taking care not to touch the log. On the opposite side the tracks spread out over a windfall of trees. "Whole family mink live here," continued Mukoki. "T'ree--mebby four--mebby five. Build trap-house right here!"

Never before had Rod seen a trap set as the old Indian now set his. Very near the end of the log over which the mink made their trail he quickly built a shelter of sticks which when completed was in the form of a tiny wigwam. At the back of this was placed a chunk of the caribou meat, and in front of this bait, so that an animal would have to spring it in passing, was set a trap, carefully covered with snow and a few leaves. Within twenty minutes Mukoki had built two of these shelters and had set two traps.

"Why do you build those little houses?" asked Rod, as they again took up their trail.

"Much snow come in winter," elucidated the Indian. "Build house to keep snow off traps. No do that, be digging out traps all winter. When mink--heem smell meat--go in house he got to go over trap. Make house for all small animal like heem.

No good for lynx. He see house--walk roun' 'n' roun' 'n' roun'--and then go 'way. Smart fellow--lynx. Wolf and fox, too."

"Is a mink worth much?"

"Fi' dollar--no less that. Seven--eight dollar for good one."

During the next mile six other mink traps were set. The creek now ran along the edge of a high rocky ridge and Mukoki's eyes began to shine with a new interest. No longer did he seem entirely absorbed in the discovery of signs of fur animals. His eyes were constantly scanning the sun-bathed side of the ridge ahead and his progress was slow and cautious. He spoke in whispers, and Rod followed his example. Frequently the two would stop and scan the openings for signs of life. Twice they set fox traps where there were evident signs of runways; in a wild ravine, strewn with tumbled trees and masses of rock, they struck a lynx track and set a trap for him at each end of the ravine; but even during these operations Mukoki's interest was divided. The hunters now walked abreast, about fifty yards apart, Rod never forging a foot ahead of the cautious Mukoki. Suddenly the youth heard a low call and he saw his companion beckoning to him with frantic enthusiasm.

"Wolf!" whispered Mukoki as Rod joined him.

In the snow were a number of tracks that reminded Rod of those made by a dog.

"T'ree wolf!" continued the Indian jubilantly. "Travel early this morning. Somewhere in warm sun on mountain!"

They followed now in the wolf trail. A little way on Rod found part of the carcass of a rabbit with fox tracks about it. Here Mukoki set another trap. A little farther still they came across a fisher trail and another trap was laid. Caribou and deer tracks crossed and recrossed the creek, but the Indian paid little attention to them. A fourth wolf joined the pack, and a fifth, and half an hour later the trail of three other wolves cut at right angles across the one they were following and disappeared in the direction of the thickly timbered plains. Mukoki's face was crinkled with joy.

"Many wolf near," he exclaimed. "Many wolf off there 'n' off there 'n' off there. Good place for night hunt."

Soon the creek swung out from the ridge and cut a circuitous channel through a small swamp. Here there were signs of wild life which set Rod's heart thumping and his blood tingling with excitement. In places the snow was literally packed with deer tracks. Trails ran in every direction, the bark had been rubbed from scores of saplings, and every step gave fresh evidence of the near presence of game. The stealth with which Mukoki now advanced was almost painful. Every twig was pressed behind him noiselessly, and once when Rod struck his snow-shoe against the butt of a small tree the old Indian held up his hands in mock horror. Ten minutes, fifteen--twenty of them passed in this cautious, breathless trailing of the swamp.

Suddenly Mukoki stopped, and a hand was held out behind him warningly. He turned his face back, and Rod knew that he saw game. Inch by inch he crouched upon his snow-shoes, and beckoned for Rod to approach, slowly, quietly. When the boy had come near enough he passed back his rifle, and his lips formed the almost noiseless word, "Shoot!"

Tremblingly Rod seized the gun and looked into the swamp ahead, Mukoki doubling down in front of him. What he saw sent him for a moment into the first nervous tremor of buck fever. Not more than a hundred yards away stood a magnificent buck browsing the tips of a clump of hazel, and just beyond him were two does. With a powerful effort Rod steadied himself. The buck was standing broadside, his head and neck stretched up, offering a beautiful shot at the vital spot behind his fore leg. At this the young hunter aimed and fired. With one spasmodic bound the animal dropped dead.

Hardly had Rod seen the effect of his shot before Mukoki was traveling swiftly toward the fallen game, unstrapping his pack as he ran. By the time the youth reached his quarry the old Indian had produced a large whisky flask holding about a quart. Without explanation he now proceeded to thrust his knife into the quivering animal's throat and fill this flask with blood. When he had finished his task he held it up with an air of unbounded satisfaction.

"Blood for wolf. Heem like blood. Smell um--come make big shoot to-night. No blood, no bait--no wolf shoot!"

Mukoki no longer maintained his usual quiet, and it was evident to Rod that the Indian considered his mission for that day practically accomplished. After taking the heart, liver and one of the hind quarters of the buck Mukoki drew a long rope of babeesh from his pack, tied one end of it around the animal's neck, flung the other end over a near limb, and with his companion's assistance hoisted the carcass until it was clear of the ground.

"If somethin' happen we no come back to-night heem safe from wolf," he explained.

The two now continued through the swamp. At its farther edge the ground rose gently from the creek toward the hills, and this sloping plain was covered with huge boulders and a thin growth of large spruce and birch. Just beyond the creek was a gigantic rock which immediately caught Mukoki's attention. All sides except one were too precipitous for ascent, and even this one could not be climbed without the assistance of a sapling or two. They could see, however, that the top of the, rock was flat, and Mukoki called attention to this fact with an exultant chuckle.

"Fine place for wolf hunt!" he exclaimed. "Many wolf off there in swamp an' in hill. We call heem here. Shoot from there!" He pointed to a clump of spruce a dozen rods away.

By Rod's watch it was now nearly noon and the two sat down to eat the sandwiches they had brought with them. Only a few minutes were lost in taking up the home trail. Beyond the swamp Mukoki cut at right angles to their trap-line until he had ascended to the top of the ridge that had been on their right and which would take them very near their camp. From this ridge Rod could look about him upon a wild and rugged scene. On one side it sloped down to the plains, but on the other it fell in almost sheer walls, forming at its base five hundred feet below a narrow and gloomy chasm, through which a small stream found its way. Several times Mukoki stopped and leaned perilously close to the dizzy edge of the mountain, peering down with critical eyes, and once when he pulled himself back cautiously by means of a small sapling he explained his interest by saying:

"Plenty bear there in spring!"

But Rod was not thinking of bears. Once more his head was filled with the thought of gold. Perhaps that very chasm held the priceless secret that had died with its owners half a century ago. The dark and gloomy silence that hung between those two walls of rock, the death-like desolation, the stealthy windings of the creek--everything in that dim and mysterious world between the two mountains, unshattered by sound and impenetrable to the winter sun, seemed in his mind to link itself with the tragedy of long ago.

Did that chasm hold the secret of the dead men?

Again and again Rod found himself asking this question as he followed Mukoki, and the oftener he asked it the nearer he seemed to an answer, until at last, with a curious, thrilling certainty that set his blood tingling he caught Mukoki by the arm and pointing back, said:

"Mukoki--the gold was found between those mountains!"

CHAPTER IX
WOLF TAKES VENGEANCE UPON HIS PEOPLE

From that hour was born in Roderick Drew's breast a strange, imperishable desire. Willingly at this moment would he have given up the winter trapping to have pursued that golden *ignis fatuus* of all ages--the lure of gold. To him the story of the old cabin, the skeletons and the treasure of the buckskin bag was complete. Those skeletons had once been men. They had found a mine--a place where they had picked up nuggets with their fingers. And that treasure ground was somewhere near. No longer was he puzzled by the fact that they had discovered no more gold in the old log cabin. In a flash he had solved that mystery. The men had just begun to gather their treasure when they had fought. What was more logical than that? One day, two, three--and they had quarreled over division, over rights. That was the time when they were most likely to quarrel. Perhaps one had discovered the gold and had therefore claimed a larger share. Anyway, the contents of the buckskin bag represented but a few days' labor. Rod was sure of that.

Mukoki had grinned and shrugged his shoulders with an air of stupendous doubt when Rod had told him that the gold lay between the mountains, so now the youth kept his thoughts to himself. It was a silent trail home. Rod's mind was too active in its new channel, and he was too deeply absorbed in impressing upon his memory certain landmarks which they passed to ask questions; and Mukoki, with the natural taciturnity of his race, seldom found occasion to break into conversation unless spoken to first. Although his eyes were constantly on the alert, Rod could see no way in which a descent could be made into the chasm from the ridge they were on. This was a little disappointing, for he had made up his mind to explore the gloomy, sunless gulch at his first opportunity. He had no doubt that Wabi would join in the adventure. Or he might take his own time, and explore it alone. He was reasonably sure that from somewhere on the opposite ridge a descent could be made into it.

Wabi was in camp when they arrived. He had set eighteen traps and had shot two spruce partridges. The birds were already cleaned for their early supper, and a thick slice of venison steak was added to the menu. During the preparation of the meal Rod described their discovery of the chasm and revealed some of his thoughts concerning it, but Wabi betrayed only passing flashes of interest. At times he seemed strangely preoccupied and would stand in an idle, contemplative mood, his hands buried deep in his pockets, while Rod or Mukoki proceeded with the little duties about the table or the stove. Finally, after arousing himself from one of these momentary spells, he pulled a brass shell from his pocket and held it out to the old Indian.

"See here," he said. "I don't want to stir up any false fears, or anything of that sort--but I found that on the trail to-day!"

Mukoki clutched at the shell as though it had been another newly found nugget of gold. The shell was empty. The lettering on the rim was still very distinct. He read ".35 Rem."

"Why, that's--"

"A shell from Rod's gun!"

For a few moments Rod and Mukoki stared at the young Indian in blank amazement.

"It's a .35 caliber Remington," continued Wabi, "and it's an auto-loading shell. There are only three guns like that in this country. I've got one, Mukoki has another--and you lost the third in your fight with the Woongas!"

The venison had begun to burn, and Mukoki quickly transferred it to the table. Without a word the three sat down to their meal.

"That means the Woongas are on our trail," declared Rod presently.

"That is what I have been trying to reason out all the afternoon," replied Wabi. "It certainly is proof that they are, or have been quite recently, on this side of the mountain. But I don't believe they know we are here. The trail I struck was about five miles from camp. It was at least two days old. Three Indians on snow-shoes were traveling north. I followed back on their trail and found after a time that the

Indians had come from the north, which leads me to believe that they were simply on a hunting expedition, cut a circle southward, and then returned to their camp. I don't believe they will come farther south. But we must keep our eyes open."

Wabi's description of the manner in which the strange trail turned gave great satisfaction to Mukoki, who nodded affirmatively when the young hunter expressed it as his belief that the Woongas would not come so far as their camp. But the discovery of their presence chilled the buoyant spirits of the hunters. There was, however, a new spice of adventure lurking in this possible peril that was not altogether displeasing, and by the time the meal was at an end something like a plan of campaign had been formed. The hunters would not wait to be attacked and then act in self-defense, possibly at a disadvantage. They would be constantly on the lookout for the Woongas, and if a fresh trail or a camp was found they would begin the man-hunt themselves.

The sun was just beginning to sink behind the distant hills in the southwest when the hunters again left camp. Wolf had received nothing to eat since the previous night, and with increasing hunger the fiery impatience lurking in his eyes and the restlessness of his movements became more noticeable. Mukoki called attention to these symptoms with a gloating satisfaction.

The gloom of early evening was enveloping the wilderness by the time the three wolf hunters reached the swamp in which Rod had slain the buck. While he carried the guns and packs, Mukoki and Wabigoon dragged the buck between them to the huge flat-top rock. Now for the first time the city youth began to understand the old pathfinder's scheme. Several saplings were cut, and by means of a long rope of babeesh the deer was dragged up the side of the rock until it rested securely upon the flat space. From the dead buck's neck the babeesh rope was now stretched across the intervening space between the rock and the clump of cedars in which the hunters were to conceal themselves. In two of these cedars, at a distance of a dozen feet from the ground, were quickly made three platforms of saplings, upon which the ambushed watchers could comfortably seat themselves. By the time complete darkness had fallen the "trap" was finished, with the exception of a detail which Rod followed with great interest.

From inside his clothes, where it had been kept warm by his body, Mukoki produced the flask of blood. A third of this blood he scattered upon the face of the rock and upon the snow at its base. The remainder he distributed, drop by drop, in trails running toward the swamp and plains.

There still remained three hours before the moon would be up, and the hunters now joined Wolf, who had been fastened half-way up the ridge. In the shelter of a big rock a small fire was built, and during their long wait the hunters passed the time away by broiling and eating chunks of venison and in going over again the events of the day.

It was nine o'clock before the moon rose above the edge of the wilderness. This great orb of the Northern night seemed to hold a never-ending fascination for Rod. It crept above the forests, a glowing, throbbing ball of red, quivering and palpitating in an effulgence that neither cloud nor mist dimmed in this desolation beyond the sphere of man; and as it rose, almost with visible movement to the eyes, the blood in it faded, until at last it seemed a great blaze of soft light between silver and gold. It was then that the whole world was lighted up under it. It was then that Mukoki, speaking softly, beckoned the others to follow him, and with Wolf at his side went down the ridge.

Making a circuit around the back of the rock, Mukoki paused near a small sapling twenty yards from the dead buck and secured Wolf by his babeesh thong. Hardly had he done so when the animal began to exhibit signs of excitement. He trotted about nervously, sniffing the air, gathering the wind from every direction, and his jaws dropped with a snarling whine. Then he struck one of the clots of blood in the snow.

"Come," whispered Wabi, pulling at Rod's sleeve, "come--quietly."

They slipped back among the shadows of the spruce and watched Wolf in unbroken silence. The animal now stood rigidly over the blood clot. His head was level with his quivering back, his ears half aslant, his nostrils pointing to a strange thrilling scent that came to him from somewhere out there in the moonlight. Once more the instinct of his breed was flooding the soul of the captive wolf. There was the odor of blood in his widening nostrils. It was not the blood of the camp, of the slaughtered game dragged in by human hands before his eyes. It was the blood of the chase!

A flashing memory of his captors turned the animal's head for an instant in backward inspection. They were gone. He could neither hear nor see them. He sniffed the sign of human presence, but that sign was always with him, and was not disturbing. The blood held him--and the strange scent, the game scent--that was coming to him more clearly every instant.

He crunched about cautiously in the snow. He found other spots of blood, and to the watchers there came a low long whine that seemed about to end in the wolf song. The blood trails were leading him away toward the game scent, and he tugged viciously at the babeesh that held him captive, gnawing at it vainly, like an angry dog, forgetting what experience had taught him many times before. Each moment added to his excitement He ran about the sapling, gulped mouthfuls of the bloody snow, and each time he paused for a moment with his open dripping jaws held toward the dead buck on the rock. The game was very near. Brute sense told him that. Oh, the longing that was in him, the twitching, quivering longing to kill--kill--kill!

He made another effort, tore up the snow in his frantic endeavors to free himself, to break loose, to follow in the wild glad cry of freed savagery in the calling of his people. He failed again, panting, whining in piteous helplessness.

Then he settled upon his haunches at the end of his babeesh thong.

For a moment his head turned to the moonlit sky, his long nose poised at right angles to the bristling hollows between his shoulders.

There came then a low, whining wail, like the beginning of the "death-song" of a husky dog--a wail that grew in length and in strength and in volume until it rose weirdly among the mountains and swept far out over the plains--the hunt call of the wolf on the trail, which calls to him the famished, gray-gaunt outlaws of the wilderness, as the bugler's notes call his fellows on the field of battle.

Three times that blood-thrilling cry went up from the captive wolf's throat, and before those cries had died away the three hunters were perched upon their platforms among the spruce.

There followed now the ominous, waiting silence of an awakened wilderness. Rod could hear his heart throbbing within him. He forgot the intense cold. His nerves tingled. He looked out over the endless plains, white and mysteriously beautiful as they lay bathed in the glow of the moon. And Wabi knew more than he what was happening. All over that wild desolation the call of the wolf had carried its meaning. Down there, where a lake lay silent in its winter sleep, a doe started in trembling and fear; beyond the mountain a huge bull moose lifted his antlered head with battle-glaring eyes; half a mile away a fox paused for an instant in its sleuth-like stalking of a rabbit; and here and there in that world of wild things the gaunt hungry people of Wolf's blood stopped in their trails and turned their heads toward the signal that was coming in wailing echoes to their ears.

And then the silence was broken. From afar--it might have been a mile away--there came an answering cry; and at that cry the wolf at the end of his babeesh thong settled upon his haunches again and sent back the call that comes only when there is blood upon the trail or when near the killing time.

There was not the rustle of a bough, not a word spoken, by the silent watchers in the spruce. Mukoki had slipped back and half lay across his support in shooting attitude. Wabi had braced a foot, and his rifle was half to his shoulder, leveled over a knee. It was Rod's turn with the big revolver, and he had practised aiming through a crotch that gave a rest to his arm.

In a few moments there came again the howl of the distant wolf on the plains, and this time it was joined by another away to the westward. And after that there came two from the plains instead of one, and then a far cry to the north and east. For the first time Rod and Wabi heard the gloating chuckle of Mukoki in his spruce a dozen feet away.

At the increasing responses of his brethren Wolf became more frantic in his efforts. The scent of fresh blood and of wounded game was becoming maddening to the captive. But his frenzy no longer betrayed itself in futile efforts to escape from the babeesh thong. Wolf knew that his cries were assembling the hunt-pack. Nearer and nearer came the responses of the leaders, and there were now only momentary rests between the deep-throated exhortations which he sent in all directions into the night.

Suddenly, almost from the swamp itself, there came a quick, excited, yelping reply, and Wabi gripped Rod by the arm.

"He has struck the place where you killed the buck," he whispered. "There'll be quick work now!"

Hardly had he spoken when a series of excited howls broke forth from the swamp, coming nearer and nearer as the hunger-crazed outlaw of the plains followed over the rich-scented trail made by the two Indians as they carried the slaughtered deer. Soon he nosed one of the trails of blood, and a moment later the watchers saw a gaunt shadow form running swiftly over the snow toward Wolf.

For an instant, as the two beasts of prey met, there fell a silence; then both animals joined in the wailing hunt-pack cry, and the wolf that was free came to the edge of the great rock and stood with his fore feet on its side, and his cry changed from that of the chase to the still more thrilling signal that told the gathering pack of game at bay.

Swiftly the wolves closed in. From over the edge of the mountain one came and joined the wolf at the rock without the hunters seeing his approach. From out of the swamp there came a pack of three, and now about the rock there grew a maddened, yelping horde, clambering and scrambling and fighting in their efforts to climb up to the game that was so near and yet beyond their reach. And sixty feet away Wolf crouched, watching the gathering of his clan, helpless, panting from his choking efforts to free himself, and quieting, gradually quieting, until in sullen silence he looked upon the scene, as though he knew the moment was very near when that thrilling spectacle would be changed into a scene of direst tragedy.

And it was Mukoki who had first said that this was the vengeance of Wolf upon his people.

From Mukoki there now came a faint hissing warning, and Wabi threw his rifle to his shoulder. There were at least a score of wolves at the base of the rock. Gradually the old Indian pulled upon the babeesh rope that led to the dead buck-- pulled until he was putting a half of his strength into the effort, and could feel the animal slowly slipping from the flat ledge. A moment more and the buck tumbled down in the midst of the waiting pack.

As flies gather upon a lump of sugar the famished animals now crowded and crushed and fought over the deer's body, and as they came thus together there sounded the quick sharp signal to fire from Mukoki.

For five seconds the edge of the spruce was a blaze of death-dealing flashes, and the deafening reports of the two rifles and the big Colt drowned the cries and struggles of the animals. When those five seconds were over fifteen shots had been fired, and five seconds later the vast, beautiful silence of the wilderness night had fallen again. About the rock was the silence of death, broken only faintly by the last gasping throes of the animals that lay dying in the snow.

In the trees there sounded the metallic clink of loading shells.

Wabi spoke first.

"I believe we did a good job, Mukoki!"

Mukoki's reply was to slip down his tree. The others followed, and hastened across to the rock. Five bodies lay motionless in the snow. A sixth was dragging himself around the side of the rock, and Mukoki attacked it with his belt-ax. Still a seventh had run for a dozen rods, leaving a crimson trail behind, and when Wabi and Rod came up to it the animal was convulsed in its last dying struggles.

"Seven!" exclaimed the Indian youth. "That is one of the best shoots we ever had. A hundred and five dollars in a night isn't bad, is it?"

The two came back to the rock, dragging the wolf with them. Mukoki was standing as rigid as a statue in the moonlight, his face turned into the north. He pointed one arm far out over the plains, and said, without turning his head,

"See!"

Far out in that silent desolation the hunters saw a lurid flash of flame. It climbed up and up, until it filled the night above it with a dull glow--a single unbroken stream of fire that rose far above the swamps and forests of the plains.

"That's a burning jackpine!" said Wabigoon.

"Burning jackpine!" agreed the old warrior. Then he added, "Woonga signal fire!"

CHAPTER X
RODERICK EXPLORES THE CHASM

To Rod the blazing pine seemed to be but a short distance away--a mile, perhaps a little more. In the silence of the two Indians as they contemplated the strange fire he read an ominous meaning. In Mukoki's eyes was a dull sullen glare, not unlike that which fills the orbs of a wild beast in a moment of deadly anger. Wabi's face was filled with an eager flush, and three times, Rod observed, he turned eyes strangely burning with some unnatural passion upon Mukoki.

Slowly, even as the instincts of his race had aroused the latent, brutish love of slaughter and the chase in the tamed wolf, the long smothered instincts of these human children of the forest began to betray themselves in their bronzed countenances. Rod watched, and he was thrilled to the soul. Back at the old cabin they had declared war upon the Woongas. Both Mukoki and Wabigoon had slipped the leashes that had long restrained them from meting first vengeance upon their enemies. Now the opportunity had come. For five minutes the great pine blazed, and then died away until it was only a smoldering tower of light. Still Mukoki gazed, speechless and grim, out into the distance of the night. At last Wabi broke the silence.

"How far away is it, Muky?"

"T'ree mile," answered the old warrior without hesitation.

"We could make it in forty minutes."

"Yes."

Wabi turned to Rod.

"You can find your way back to camp alone, can't you?" he asked.

"Not if you're going over there!" declared the white boy. "I'm going with you."

Mukoki broke in upon them with a harsh disappointed laugh.

"No go. No go over there." He spoke with emphasis, and shook his head. "We lose pine in five minutes. No find Woonga camp--make big trail for Woongas to see in morning. Better wait. Follow um trail in day, then shoot!"

Rod found immense relief in the old Indian's decision. He did not fear a fight; in fact, he was a little too anxious to meet the outlaws who had stolen his gun, now that they had determined upon opening fire on sight. But in this instance he was possessed of the cooler judgment of his race. He believed that as yet the Woongas were not aware of their presence in this region, and that there was still a large possibility of the renegades traveling northward beyond their trapping sphere. He hoped that this would be the case, in spite of his desire to recapture his gun. A scrimmage with the Woongas just now would spoil the plans he had made for discovering gold.

The "Skeleton Mine," as he had come to call it, now absorbed his thoughts beyond everything else. He felt confident that he would discover the lost treasure ground if given time, and he was just as confident that if war was once begun between themselves and the Woongas it would mean disaster or quick flight from the country. Even Wabi, worked up more in battle enthusiasm than by gold fever, conceded that if half of the Woongas were in this country they were much too powerful for them to cope with successfully, especially as one of them was without a rifle.

It was therefore with inward exultation that Rod saw the project of attack dropped and Mukoki and Wabigoon proceed with their short task of scalping the seven wolves. During this operation Wolf was allowed to feast upon the carcass of the buck.

That night there was but little sleep in the old cabin. It was two o'clock when the hunters arrived in camp and from that hour until nearly four they sat about the hot stove making plans for the day that was nearly at hand. Rod could but contrast the excitement that had now taken possession of them with the tranquil joy with which they had first taken up their abode in this dip in the hilltop. And how different were their plans from those of two or three days ago! Not one of them now but realized their peril. They were in an ideal hunting range, but it was evidently very near, if not actually in, the Woonga country. At any moment they might be forced to fight for their lives or abandon their camp, and perhaps they would be compelled to do both.

So the gathering about the stove was in reality a small council of war. It was decided that the old cabin should immediately be put into a condition of defense, with a loophole on each side, strong new bars at the door, and with a thick barricade near at hand that could be quickly fitted against the window in case of attack. Until the war-clouds cleared away, if they cleared at all, the camp would be continually guarded by one of the hunters, and with this garrison would be left both of the heavy revolvers. At dawn or a little later Mukoki would set out upon Wabi's trap-line, both to become acquainted with it and to extend the line of traps, while later in the day the Indian youth would follow Mukoki's line, visiting the houses already built and setting other traps. This scheme left to Rod the first day's watch in camp.

Mukoki aroused himself from his short sleep with the first approach of dawn but did not awaken his tired companions until breakfast was ready. When the meal was finished he seized his gun and signified his intention of visiting the mink traps just beyond the hill before leaving on his long day's trail. Rod at once joined him, leaving Wabi to wash the dishes.

They were shortly within view of the trap-houses near the creek. Instinctively the eyes of both rested upon these houses and neither gave very close attention to the country ahead or about them. As a result both were exceedingly startled when they heard a huge snort and a great crunching in the deep snow close beside them. From out of a small growth of alders had dashed a big bull moose, who was now tearing with the speed of a horse up the hillside toward the hidden camp, evidently seeking the quick shelter of the dip.

"Wait heem git top of hill!" shouted Mukoki, swinging his rifle to his shoulder. "Wait!"

It was a beautiful shot and Rod was tempted to ignore the old Indian's advice. But he knew that there was some good reason for it, so he held his trembling finger. Hardly had the animal's huge antlered head risen to the sky-line when Mukoki shouted again, and the young hunter pressed the trigger of his automatic gun three times in rapid succession. It was a short shot, not more than two hundred yards, and Mukoki fired but once just as the bull mounted the hilltop.

The next instant the moose was gone and Rod was just about to dash in pursuit when his companion caught him by the arm.

"We got um!" he grinned. "He run downhill, then fall--ver' close to camp. Ver' good scheme--wait heem git on top hill. No have to carry meat far!"

As coolly as though nothing had occurred the Indian turned again in the direction of the traps. Rod stood as though he had been nailed to the spot, his mouth half open in astonishment.

"We go see traps," urged Mukoki. "Find moose dead when we go back."

But Roderick Drew, who had hunted nothing larger than house rats in his own city, was not the young man to see the logic of this reasoning, and before Mukoki could open his mouth again he was hurrying up the hill. On its summit he saw a huge torn-up blotch in the snow, spattered with blood, where the moose had fallen first after the shots; and at the foot of the hill, as the Indian had predicted, the great animal lay dead.

Wabi was hastening across the lake, attracted by the shots, and both reached the slain bull at about the same time. Rod quickly perceived that three shots had taken effect; one, which was undoubtedly Mukoki's carefully directed ball, in a vital spot behind the fore leg, and two through the body. The fact that two of his own shots had taken good effect filled the white youth with enthusiasm, and he was still gesticulating excitedly in describing the bull's flight to Wabi when the old Indian came over the hill, grinning broadly, and holding up for their inspection a magnificent mink.

The day could not have begun more auspiciously for the hunters, and by the time Mukoki was ready to leave upon his long trail the adventurers were in buoyant spirits, the distressing fears of the preceding night being somewhat dispelled by their present good fortune and the glorious day which now broke in full splendor upon the wilderness.

Until their early dinner Wabi remained in camp, securing certain parts of the moose and assisting Rod in putting the cabin into a state of defense according to their previous plans. It was not yet noon when he started over Mukoki's trap-line.

Left to his own uninterrupted thoughts, Rod's mind was once more absorbed in his scheme of exploring the mysterious chasm. He had noticed during his inspection from the top of the ridge that the winter snows had as yet fallen but little in the gloomy gulch between the mountains, and he was eager to attempt his adventure before other snows came or the fierce blizzards of December filled the chasm with drifts. Later in the afternoon he brought forth the buckskin bag from a niche in the log wall where it had been concealed, and one after another carefully examined the golden nuggets. He found, as he had expected, that they were worn to exceeding smoothness, and that every edge had been dulled and rounded. Rod's favorite study in school had been a minor branch of geology and mineralogy, and he knew that only running water could work this smoothness. He was therefore confident that the nuggets had been discovered in or on the edge of a running stream. And that stream, he was sure, was the one in the chasm.

But Rod's plans for an early investigation were doomed to disappointment. Late that day both Mukoki and Wabi returned, the latter with a red fox and another mink, the former with a fisher, which reminded Rod of a dog just growing out of puppyhood, and another story of strange trails that renewed their former apprehensions. The old Indian had discovered the remnants of the burned jackpine, and about it were the snow-shoe tracks of three Indians. One of these trails came from the north and two from the west, which led him to believe that the pine had been fired as a signal to call the two. At the very end of their trap-line, which extended about four miles from camp, a single snow-shoe trail had cut across at right angles, also swinging into the north.

These discoveries necessitated a new arrangement of the plans that had been made the preceding night. Hereafter, it was agreed, only one trap-line would be visited each day, and by two of the hunters in company, both armed with rifles. Rod saw that this meant the abandonment of his scheme for exploring the chasm, at least for the present.

Day after day now passed without evidences of new trails, and each day added to the hopes of the adventurers that they were at last to be left alone in the country. Never had Mukoki or Wabigoon been in a better trapping ground, and every visit to their lines added to their hoard of furs. If left unmolested it was plainly evident that they would take a small fortune back to Wabinosh House with them early in the spring. Besides many mink, several fisher, two red foxes and a lynx, they added two fine "cross" foxes and three wolf scalps to their treasure during the next three weeks. Rod began to think occasionally of the joy their success would bring to the little home hundreds of miles away, where he knew that the mother was waiting and praying for him every day of her life; and there were times, too, when he found himself counting the days that must still elapse before he returned to Minnetaki and the Post.

But at no time did he give up his determination to explore the chasm. From the first Mukoki and Wabigoon had regarded this project with little favor, declaring the impossibility of discovering gold under snow, even though gold was there; so Rod waited and watched for an opportunity to make the search alone, saying nothing about his plans.

On a beautiful day late in December, when the sun rose with dazzling brightness, his opportunity came. Wabi was to remain in camp, and Mukoki, who was again of the belief that they were safe from the Woongas, was to follow one of the trap-lines alone. Supplying himself well with food, taking Wabi's rifle, a double allowance of cartridges, a knife, belt-ax, and a heavy blanket in his pack, Rod set out for the chasm. Wabi laughed as he stood in the doorway to see him off.

"Good luck to you, Rod; hope you find gold," he cried gaily, waving a final good-by with his hand.

"If I don't return to-night don't you fellows worry about me," called back the youth. "If things look promising I may camp in the chasm and take up the hunt again in the morning."

He now passed quickly to the second ridge, knowing from previous experience that it would be impossible to make a descent into the gulch from the first mountain. This range, a mile south of the camp, had not been explored by the hunters, but Rod was sure that there was no danger of losing himself as long as he followed along the edge of the chasm which was in itself a constant and infallible guide. Much to his disappointment he found that the southern walls of this mysterious break between the mountains were as precipitous as those on the opposite side, and for two hours he looked in vain for a place where he might climb down. The country was now becoming densely wooded and he was constantly encountering signs of big game. But he paid little attention to these. Finally he came to a point where the forest swept over and down the steep side of the mountain, and to his great joy he saw that by strapping his snow-shoes to his back and making good use of his hands it was possible for him to make a descent.

Fifteen minutes later, breathless but triumphant, he stood at the bottom of the chasm. On his right rose the strip of cedar forest; on his left he was shut in by towering walls of black and shattered rock. At his feet was the little stream which had played such an important part in his golden dreams, frozen in places, and in others kept clear of ice by the swiftness of its current. A little ahead of him was that gloomy, sunless part of the chasm into which he had peered so often from the top of the ridge on the north. As he advanced step by step into its mysterious silence, his eyes alert, his nerves stretched to a tension of the keenest expectancy, there crept over him a feeling that he was invading that enchanted territory which, even at this moment, might be guarded by the spirits of the two mortals who had died because of the treasure it held.

Narrower and narrower became the walls high over his head. Not a ray of sunlight penetrated into the soundless gloom. Not a leaf shivered in the still air. The creek gurgled and spattered among its rocks, without the note of a bird or the chirp of a squirrel to interrupt its monotony. Everything was dead. Now and then Rod could hear the wind whispering over the top of the chasm. But not a breath of it came down to him. Under his feet was only sufficient snow to deaden his own footsteps, and he still carried his snow-shoes upon his back.

Suddenly, from the thick gloom that hung under one of the cragged walls, there came a thundering, unearthly sound that made him stop, his rifle swung half to shoulder. He saw that he had disturbed a great owl, and passed on. Now and then he paused beside the creek and took up handful after handful of its pebbles, his heart beating high with hope at every new gleam he caught among them, and never sinking to disappointment though he found no gold. The gold was here--somewhere. He was as certain of that as he was of the fact that he was living, and searching for it. Everything assured him of that; the towering masses of cleft rock, whole walls seeming about to crumble into ruin, the broad margins of pebbles along the creek--everything, to the very stillness and mystery in the air, spoke this as the abode of the skeletons' secret. It was this inexplicable *something*--this unseen, mysterious element hovering in the air that caused the white youth to advance step by step, silently, cautiously, as though the slightest sound under his feet might awaken the deadliest of enemies. And it was because of this stealth in his progress that he came very close upon something that was living, and without startling it. Less than fifty yards ahead of him he saw an object moving slowly among the rocks. It was a fox. Even before the animal had detected his presence he had aimed and fired.

Thunderous echoes rose up about him. They rolled down the chasm, volume upon volume, until in the ghostly gloom between the mountain walls he stood and listened, a nervous shiver catching him once or twice. Not until the last echo had died away did he approach where the fox lay upon the snow. It was not red. It was not black. It was not--

His heart gave a big excited thump. The bleeding creature at his feet was the most beautiful animal he had ever seen--and the tip of its thick black fur was silver gray.

Then, in that lonely chasm, there went up a great human whoop of joy.

"A silver fox!"

Rod spoke the words aloud. For five minutes he stood and looked upon his prize. He held it up and stroked it, and from what Wabi and Mukoki had told him he knew that the silken pelt of this creature was worth more to them than all the furs at the camp together. He made no effort to skin it, but put the animal in his pack and resumed his slow, noiseless exploration of the gulch.

He had now passed beyond those points in the range from which he had looked down into this narrow, shut-in world. Ever more wild and gloomy became the chasm. At times the two walls of rock seemed almost to meet far above his head; under gigantic, overhanging crags there lurked the shadows of night. Fascinated by the grandeur and loneliness of the scenes through which he was passing Rod forgot the travel of time. Mile after mile he continued his tireless trail. He had no inclination to eat. He stopped only once at the creek to drink. And when he looked at his watch he was astonished to find that it was three o'clock in the afternoon.

It was now too late to think of returning to camp. Within an hour the day gloom of the chasm would be thickening into that of night. So Rod stopped at the first good camp site, threw off his pack, and proceeded with the building of a cedar shelter. Not until this was completed and a sufficient supply of wood for the night's fire was at hand did he begin getting supper. He had brought a pail with him and soon the appetizing odors of boiling coffee and broiling moose sirloin filled the air.

Night had fallen between the mountain walls by the time Rod sat down to his meal.

CHAPTER XI
RODERICK'S DREAM

A chilling loneliness now crept over the young adventurer. Even as he ate he tried to peer out into the mysterious darkness. A sound from up the chasm, made by some wild prowler of the night, sent a nervous tremor through him. He was not afraid; he would not have confessed to that. But still, the absolute, almost gruesome silence between the two mountains, the mere knowledge that he was alone in a place where the foot of man had not trod for more than half a century, was not altogether quieting to his nerves. What mysteries might not these grim walls hold? What might not happen here, where everything was so strange, so weird, and so different from the wilderness world just over the range?

Rod tried to laugh away his nervousness, but the very sound of his own voice was distressing. It rose in unnatural shivering echoes--a low, hollow mockery of a laugh beating itself against the walls; a ghost of a laugh, Rod thought, and that very thought made him hunch closer to the fire. The young hunter was not superstitious, or at least he was not unnaturally so; but what man or boy is there in this whole wide world of ours who does not, at some time, inwardly cringe from something in the air--something that does not exist and never did exist, but which holds a peculiar and nameless fear for the soul of a human being?

And Rod, as he piled his fire high with wood and shrank in the warmth of his cedar shelter, felt that nameless dread; and there came to him no thought of sleep, no feeling of fatigue, but only that he was alone, absolutely alone, in the mystery and almost unending silence of the chasm. Try as he would he could not keep from his mind the vision of the skeletons as he had first seen them in the old cabin.

Many, many years ago, even before his own mother was born, those skeletons had trod this very chasm. They had drunk from the same creek as he, they had clambered over the same rocks, they had camped perhaps where he was camping now! They, too, in flesh and life, had strained their ears in the grim silence, they had watched the flickering light of their camp-fire on the walls of rock--and they had found gold!

Just now, if Rod could have moved himself by magic, he would have been safely back in camp. He listened. From far back over the trail he had followed there came a lonely, plaintive, almost pleading cry.

"'Ello--'ello--'ello!"

It sounded like a distant human greeting, but Rod knew that it was the awakening night cry of what Wabi called the "man owl." It was weirdly human-like; and the echoes came softly, and more softly, until ghostly voices seemed to be whispering in the blackness about him.

"'Ello--'ello--'ello!"

The boy shivered and laid his rifle across his knees. There was tremendous comfort in the rifle. Rod fondled it with his fingers, and two or three times he felt as though he would almost like to talk to it. Only those who have gone far into the silence and desolation of the unblazed wilderness know just how human a good rifle becomes to its owner. It is a friend every hour of the night and day, faithful to its master's desires, keeping starvation at bay and holding death for his enemies; a guaranty of safety at his bedside by night, a sharp-fanged watch-dog by day, never treacherous and never found wanting by the one who bestows upon it the care of a comrade and friend. Thus had Rod come to look upon his rifle. He rubbed the barrel now with his mittens; he polished the stock as he sat in his loneliness, and long afterward, though he had determined to remain awake during the night, he fell asleep with it clasped tightly in his hands.

It was an uneasy, troubled slumber in which the young adventurer's visions and fears took a more realistic form. He half sat, half lay, upon his cedar boughs; his head fell forward upon his breast, his feet were stretched out to the fire. Now and then unintelligible sounds fell from his lips, and he would start suddenly as if about to awaken, but each time would sink back into his restless sleep, still clutching the gun.

The visions in his head began to take a more definite form. Once more he was on the trail, and had come to the old cabin. But this time he was alone. The window of the cabin was wide open, but the door was tightly closed, just as the hunters had found it when they first came down into the dip. He approached cautiously. When very near the window he heard sounds--strange sounds--like the clicking of bones!

Step by step in his dream he approached the window and looked in. And there he beheld a sight that froze him to the marrow. Two huge skeletons were struggling in deadly embrace. He could hear no sound but the click-click-click of their bones. He saw the gleam of knives held between fleshless fingers, and he saw now that both were struggling for the possession of something that was upon the table. Now one almost reached it, now the other, but neither gained possession.

The clicking of the bones became louder, the struggle fiercer, the knives of the skeleton combatants rose and fell. Then one staggered back and sank in a heap on the floor.

For a moment the victor swayed, tottered to the table, and gripped the mysterious object in its bony fingers.

As it stumbled weakly against the cabin wall the gruesome creature held the object up, and Rod saw that it was a roll of birch-bark!

An ember in the dying fire snapped with a sound like the report of a small pistol and Rod sat bolt upright, awake, staring, trembling. What a horrible dream! He drew in his cramped legs and approached the fire on his knees, holding his rifle in one hand while he piled on wood with the other.

What a horrible dream!

He shuddered and ran his eyes around the impenetrable wall of blackness that shut him in, the thought constantly flashing through his mind, what a horrible dream--what a horrible dream!

He sat down again and watched the flames of his fire as they climbed higher and higher. The light and the heat cheered him, and after a little he allowed his mind to dwell upon the adventure of his slumber. It had made him sweat. He took off his cap and found that the hair about his forehead was damp.

All the different phases of a dream return to one singly when awake, and it was with the suddenness of a shot that there came to Rod a remembrance of the skeleton hand held aloft, clutching between its gleaming fleshless fingers the roll of birch-bark. And with that memory of his dream there came another--the skeleton in the cabin was clutching a piece of birch-bark when they had buried it!

Could that crumpled bit of bark hold the secret of the lost mine?

Was it for the possession of that bark instead of the buckskin bag that the men had fought and died?

As the minutes passed Rod forgot his loneliness, forgot his nervousness and only thought of the possibilities of the new clue that had come to him in a dream. Wabi and Mukoki had seen the bark clutched in the skeleton fingers, but they as well as he had given it no special significance, believing that it had been caught up in some terrible part of the struggle when both combatants were upon the floor, or perhaps in the dying agonies of the wounded man against the wall. Rod remembered now that they had found no more birch-bark upon the floor, which they would have done if a supply had been kept there for kindling fires. Step by step he went over the search they had made in the old cabin, and more and more satisfied did he become that the skeleton hand held something of importance for them.

He replenished his fire and waited impatiently for dawn. At four o'clock, before day had begun to dispel the gloom of night, he cooked his breakfast and prepared his pack for the homeward journey. Soon afterward a narrow rim of light broke through the rift in the chasm. Slowly it crept downward, until the young hunter could make out objects near him and the walls of the mountains.

Thick shadows still defied his vision when he began retracing his steps over the trail he had made the day before. He returned with the same caution that he had used in his advance. Even more carefully, if possible, did he scrutinize the rocks and the creek ahead. He had already found life in the chasm, and he might find more.

The full light of day came quickly now, and with it the youth's progress became more rapid. He figured that if he lost no time in further investigation of the creek he would arrive at camp by noon, and they would dig up the skeleton without delay. There was little snow in the chasm, in spite of the lateness of the season, and if the roll of bark held the secret of the lost gold it would be possible for them to locate the treasure before other snows came to baffle them.

At the spot where he had killed the silver fox Rod paused for a moment. He wondered if foxes ever traveled in pairs, and regretted that he had not asked Wabi or Mukoki that question. He could see where the fox had come straight from the black wall of the mountain. Curiosity led him over the trail. He had not followed it more than two hundred yards when he stopped in sudden astonishment. Plainly marked in the snow before him was the trail of a pair of snow-shoes! Whoever had been there had passed since he shot the fox, for the imprints of the animal's feet were buried under those of the snow-shoes.

Who was the other person in the chasm?

Was it Wabi?

Had Mukoki or he come to join him? Or--

He looked again at the snow-shoe trail. It was a peculiar trail, unlike the one made by his own shoes. The imprints were a foot longer than his own, and narrower. Neither Wabi nor Mukoki wore shoes that would make that trail!

At this point the strange trail had turned and disappeared among the rocks along the wall of the mountain, and it occurred to Rod that perhaps the stranger had not discovered his presence in the chasm. There was some consolation in this thought, but it was doomed to quick disappointment. Very cautiously the youth advanced, his rifle held in readiness and his eyes searching every place of concealment ahead of him. A hundred yards farther on the stranger had stopped, and from the way in which the snow was packed Rod knew that he had stood in a listening and watchful attitude for some time. From this point the trail took another turn and came down until, from behind a huge rock, the stranger had cautiously peered out upon the path made by the white youth.

It was evident that he was extremely anxious to prevent the discovery of his own trail, for now the mysterious spy threaded his way behind rocks until he had again come to the shelter of the mountain wall.

Rod was perplexed. He realized the peril of his dilemma, and yet he knew not what course to take to evade it. He had little doubt that the trail was made by one of the treacherous Woongas, and that the Indian not only knew of his presence, but was somewhere in the rocks ahead of him, perhaps even now waiting behind some ambuscade to shoot him. Should he follow the trail, or would it be safer to steal along among the rocks of the opposite wall of the chasm?

He had decided upon the latter course when his eyes caught a narrow horizontal slit cleaving the face of the mountain on his left, toward which the snow-shoe tracks seemed to lead. With his rifle ready for instant use the youth slowly approached the fissure, and was surprised to find that it was a complete break in the wall of rock, not more than four feet wide, and continuing on a steady incline to the summit of the ridge. At the mouth of this fissure his mysterious watcher had taken off his snow-shoes and Rod could see where he had climbed up the narrow exit from the chasm.

With a profound sense of relief the young hunter hurried along the base of the mountain, keeping well within its shelter so that eyes that might be spying from above could not see his movements. He now felt no fear of danger. The stranger's flight up the cleft in the chasm wall and his careful attempts to conceal his trail among the rocks assured Rod that he had no designs upon his life. His chief purpose had seemed to be to keep secret his own presence in the gorge, and this fact in itself added to the mystification of the white youth. For a long time he had been secretly puzzled, and had evolved certain ideas of his own because of the movements of the Woongas. Contrary to the opinions of Mukoki and Wabigoon, he believed that the red outlaws were perfectly conscious of their presence in the dip. From the first their actions had been unaccountable, but not once had one of their snow-shoe trails crossed their trap-lines.

Was this fact in itself not significant? Rod was of a contemplative theoretical turn of mind, one of those wide-awake, interesting young fellows who find food for conjecture in almost every incident that occurs, and his suspicions were now aroused to an unusual pitch. A chief fault, however, was that he kept most of his suspicions to himself, for he believed that Mukoki and Wabigoon, born and taught in the life of the wilderness, were infallible in their knowledge of the ways and the laws and the perils of the world they were in.

CHAPTER XII
THE SECRET OF THE SKELETON'S HAND

A little before noon Rod arrived at the top of the hill from which he could look down on their camp. He was filled with pleasurable anticipation, and with an unbounded swelling satisfaction that caused him to smile as he proceeded into the dip. He had found a fortune in the mysterious chasm. The burden of the silver fox upon his shoulders was a most pleasing reminder of that, and he pictured the moment when the good-natured raillery of Mukoki and Wabigoon would be suddenly turned into astonishment and joy.

As he approached the cabin the young hunter tried to appear disgusted and half sick, and his effort was not bad in spite of his decided inclination to laugh. Wabi met him in the doorway, grinning broadly, and Mukoki greeted him with a throatful of his inimitable chuckles.

"Aha, here's Rod with a packful of gold!" cried the young Indian, striking an expectant attitude. "Will you let us see the treasure?" In spite of his banter there was gladness in his face at Rod's arrival.

The youth threw off his pack with a spiritless effort and flopped into a chair as though in the last stage of exhaustion.

"You'll have to undo the pack," he replied. "I'm too tired and hungry."

Wabi's manner changed at once to one of real sympathy.

"I'll bet you're tired, Rod, and half starved. We'll have dinner in a hurry. Ho, Muky, put on the steak, will you?"

There followed a rattle of kettles and tin pans and the Indian youth gave Rod a glad slap on the back as he hurried to the table. He was evidently in high spirits, and burst into a snatch of song as he cut up a loaf of bread.

"I'm tickled to see you back," he admitted, "for I was getting a little bit nervous.

We had splendid luck on our lines yesterday. Brought in another 'cross' and three mink. Did you see anything?"

"Aren't you going to look in the pack?"

Wabi turned and gazed at his companion with a half-curious hesitating smile.

"Anything in it?" he asked suspiciously.

"See here, boys," cried Rod, forgetting himself in his suppressed enthusiasm. "I said there was a treasure in that chasm, and there was. I found it. You are welcome to look into that pack if you wish!"

Wabi dropped the knife with which he was cutting the bread and went to the pack. He touched it with the toe of his boot, lifted it in his hands, and glanced at Rod again.

"It isn't a joke?" he asked.

"No."

Rod turned his back upon the scene and began to take off his coat as coolly as though it were the commonest thing in the world for him to bring silver foxes into camp. Only when Wabi gave a suppressed yell did he turn about, and then he found the Indian standing erect and holding out the silver to the astonished gaze of Mukoki.

"Is it a good one?" he asked.

"A beauty!" gasped Wabi.

Mukoki had taken the animal and was examining it with the critical eyes of a connoisseur.

"Ver' fine!" he said. "At Post heem worth fi' hundred dollars--at Montreal t'ree hundred more!"

Wabi strode across the cabin and thrust out his hand.

"Shake, Rod!"

As the two gripped hands he turned to Mukoki.

"Bear witness, Mukoki, that this young gentleman is no longer a tenderfoot. He has shot a silver fox. He has done a whole winter's work in one day. I take off my hat to you, Mr. Drew!"

Roderick's face reddened with a flush of pleasure.

"And that isn't all, Wabi," he said. His eyes were filled with a sudden intense earnestness, and in the strangeness of the change Wabi forgot to loosen the grip of his fingers about his companion's hand.

"You don't mean that you found--"

"No, I didn't find gold," anticipated Rod. "But the gold is there! I know it. And I think I have found a clue. You remember that when you and I examined the skeleton against the wall we saw that it clutched something that looked like birch-bark in its hand? Well, I believe that birch-bark holds the key to the lost mine!"

Mukoki had come beside them and stood listening to Rod, his face alive with keen interest. In Wabi's eyes there was a look half of doubt, half of belief.

"It might," he said slowly. "It wouldn't do any harm to see."

He stepped to the stove and took off the partly cooked steak. Rod slipped on his coat and hat and Mukoki seized his belt-ax and the shovel. No words were spoken, but there was a mutual understanding that the investigation was to precede dinner. Wabi was silent and thoughtful and Rod could see that his suggestion had at least made a deep impression upon him. Mukoki's eyes began to gleam again with the old fire with which he had searched the cabin for gold.

The skeletons were buried only a few inches deep in the frozen earth in the edge of the cedar forest, and Mukoki soon exposed them to view. Almost the first object that met their eyes was the skeleton hand clutching its roll of birch-bark. It was Rod who dropped upon his knees to the gruesome task.

With a shudder at the touch of the cold bones he broke the fingers back. One of them snapped with a sharp sound, and as he rose with the bark in his hand his face was bloodlessly white. The bones were covered again and the three returned to the cabin.

Still silent, they gathered about the table. With age the bark of the birch hardens and rolls itself tightly, and the piece Rod held was almost like thin steel. Inch by inch it was spread out, cracking and snapping in brittle protest. The hunters could see that the bark was in a single unbroken strip about ten inches long by six in width. Two inches, three, four were unrolled--and still the smooth surface was blank. Another half-inch, and the bark refused to unroll farther.

"Careful!" whispered Wabi.

With the point of his knife he loosened the cohesion.

"I guess--there's--nothing--" began Rod.

Even as he spoke he caught his breath. A mark had appeared on the bark, a black, meaningless mark with a line running down from it into the scroll.

Another fraction of an inch and the line was joined by a second, and then with an unexpectedness that was startling the remainder of the roll released itself like a spring--and to the eyes of the three wolf hunters was revealed the secret of the skeleton hand.

Spread out before them was a map, or at least what they at once accepted as a map, though in reality it was more of a crude diagram of straight and crooked lines, with here and there a partly obliterated word to give it meaning. In several places there were mere evidences of words, now entirely illegible. But what first held the attention of Rod and his companions were several lines in writing under the rough sketch on the bark, still quite plain, which formed the names of three men. Roderick read them aloud.

"John Ball, Henri Langlois, Peter Plante."

Through the name of John Ball had been drawn a broad black line which had almost destroyed the letters, and at the end of this line, in brackets, was printed a word in French which Wabi quickly translated.

"Dead!" he breathed. "The Frenchmen killed him!"

The words shot from him in hot excitement.

Rod did not reply. Slowly he drew a trembling finger over the map. The first word he encountered was unintelligible. Of the next he could only make out one letter, which gave him no clue. Evidently the map had been made with a different and less durable substance than that with which the names had been written. He followed down the first straight black line, and where this formed a junction with a wider crooked line were two words quite distinct:

"Second waterfall."

Half an inch below this Rod could make out the letters T, D and L, widely scattered.

"That's the third waterfall," he exclaimed eagerly.

At this point the crude lines of the diagram stopped, and immediately below, between the map and the three names, it was evident that there had been considerable writing. But not a word of it could the young hunters make out. That writing, without doubt, had given the key to the lost gold. Rod looked up, his face betraying the keenness of his disappointment. He knew that under his hand he held all that was left of the secret of a great treasure. But he was more baffled than ever. Somewhere in this vast desolation there were three waterfalls, and somewhere near the third waterfall the Englishman and the two Frenchmen had found their gold. That was all he knew. He had not found a waterfall in the chasm; they had not discovered one in all their trapping and hunting excursions.

Wabi was looking down into his face in silent thought. Suddenly he reached out and seized the sheet of bark and examined it closely. As he looked there came a deeper flush in his face, his eyes brightened and he gave a cry of excitement.

"By George, I believe we can peel this!" he cried. "See here, Muky!" He thrust the birch under the old Indian's eyes. Even Mukoki's hands were trembling.

"Birch-bark is made up of a good many layers, each as thin as the thinnest paper," he explained to Rod as Mukoki continued his examination. "If we can peel off that first layer, and then hold it up to the light, we shall be able to see the impression of every word that was ever made on it--even though they were written a hundred years ago!"

Mukoki had gone to the door, and now he turned, grinning exultantly.

"She peel!"

He showed them where he had stripped back a corner of the film-like layer. Then he sat down in the light, his head bent over, and for many minutes he worked at his tedious task while Wabi and Rod hung back in soundless suspense. Half an hour later Mukoki straightened himself, rose to his feet and held out the precious film to Rod.

As tenderly as though his own life depended upon its care, Rod held the piece of birch, now a silken, almost transparent sheet, between himself and the light. A cry welled up into his throat. It was repeated by Wabi. And then there was silence--a silence broken only by their bated breaths and the excited thumpings of their hearts.

As though they had been written but yesterday, the mysterious words on the map were disclosed to their eyes. Where Rod had made out only three letters there were now plainly discernible the two words "third waterfall," and very near to these was the word "cabin." Below them were several lines, clearly impressed in the birch film. Slowly, his voice trembling, Rod read them to his companions.

"We, John Ball, Henri Langlois, and Peter Plante, having discovered gold at this fall, do hereby agree to joint partnership in the same, and do pledge ourselves to forget our past differences and work in mutual good will and honesty, so help us God. Signed,

"JOHN BALL, HENRI LANGLOIS, PETER PLANTE."

At the very top of the map the impression of several other words caught Rod's eyes. They were more indistinct than any of the others, but one by one he made them out. A hot blurring film seemed to fall over his eyes and he felt as though his heart had suddenly come up into his throat. Wabi's breath was burning against his cheek, and it was Wabi who spoke the words aloud.

"Cabin and head of chasm."

Rod went back to the table and sat down, the precious bit of birch-bark under his hand. Mukoki, standing mute, had listened and heard, and was as if stunned by their discovery. But now his mind returned to the moose steak, and he placed it on the stove. Wabi stood with his hands in his pockets, and after a little he laughed a trembling, happy laugh.

"Well, Rod, you've found your mine. You are as good as rich!"

"You mean that we have found our mine," corrected the white youth. "We are three, and we just naturally fill the places of John Ball, Henri Langlois and Peter Plante. They are all dead. The gold is ours!"

Wabi had taken up the map.

"I can't see the slightest possibility of our not finding it," he said. "The directions are as plain as day. We follow the chasm, and somewhere in that chasm we come to a waterfall. A little beyond this the creek that runs through the gorge empties into a larger stream, and we follow this second creek or river until we come to the third fall. The cabin is there, and the gold can not be far away."

He had carried the map to the door again, and Rod joined him.

"There is nothing that gives us an idea of distance on the map," he continued. "How far did you travel down the chasm?"

"Ten miles, at least," replied Rod.

"And you discovered no fall?"

"No."

With a splinter picked up from the floor Wabi measured the distances between the different points on the diagram.

"There is no doubt but what this map was drawn by John Ball," he said after a few moments of silent contemplation. "Everything points to that fact. Notice that all of the writing is in one hand, except the signatures of Langlois and Plante, and you could hardly decipher the letters in those signatures if you did not already know their names from this writing below. Ball wrote a good hand, and from the construction of the agreement over the signatures he was a man of pretty fair education. Don't you think so? Well, he must have drawn this map with some idea of distance in his mind. The second fall is only half as far from the first fall as the third fall is from the second, which seems to me conclusive evidence of this. If he had not had distance in mind he would not have separated the falls in this way on the map."

"Then if we can find the first fall we can figure pretty nearly how far the last fall is from the head of the chasm," said Rod.

"Yes. I believe the distance from here to the first fall will give us a key to the whole thing."

Rod had produced a pencil from one of his pockets and was figuring on the smooth side of a chip.

"The gold is a long way from here at the best, Wabi. I explored the chasm for ten miles. Say that we find the first fall within fifteen miles. Then, according to the map, the second fall would be about twenty miles from the first, and the third forty miles from the second. If the first fall is within fifteen miles of this cabin the third fall is at least seventy-five miles away."

Wabi nodded.

"But we may not find the first fall within that distance," he said. "By George--" He stopped and looked at Rod with an odd look of doubt in his face. "If the gold is seventy-five or a hundred miles away, why were those men here, and with only a handful of nuggets in their possession? Is it possible that the gold played out--that they found only what was in the buckskin bag?"

"If that were so, why should they have fought to the death for the possession of the map?" argued Rod.

Mukoki was turning the steak. He had not spoken, but now he said:

"Mebby going to Post for supplies."

"That's exactly what they were doing!" shouted the Indian youth. "Muky, you have solved the whole problem. They were going for supplies. And they didn't fight for the map--not for the map alone!"

His face flushed with new excitement.

"Perhaps I am wrong, but it all seems clear to me now," he continued. "Ball and the two Frenchmen worked their find until they ran out of supplies. Wabinosh House is over a hundred years old, and fifty years ago that was the nearest point where they could get more. In some way it fell to the Frenchmen to go. They had probably accumulated a hoard of gold, and before they left they murdered Ball. They brought with them only enough gold to pay for their supplies, for it was their purpose not to arouse the suspicion of any adventurers who happened to be at the Post. They could easily have explained their possession of those few nuggets. In this cabin either Langlois or Plante tried to kill his companion, and thus become the sole possessor of the treasure, and the fight, fatal to both, ensued. I may be wrong, but--by George, I believe that is what happened!"

"And that they buried the bulk of their gold somewhere back near the third fall?"

"Yes; or else they brought the gold here and buried it somewhere near this very cabin!"

They were interrupted by Mukoki.

"Dinner ready!" he called.

CHAPTER XIII
SNOWED IN

Until the present moment Rod had forgotten to speak of the mysterious man-trail he had encountered in the chasm. The excitement of the past hour had made him oblivious to all other things, but now as they ate their dinner he described the strange maneuvers of the spying Woonga. He did not, however, voice those fears which had come to him in the gorge, preferring to allow Mukoki and Wabigoon to draw their own conclusions. By this time the two Indians were satisfied that the Woongas were not contemplating attack, but that for some unaccountable reason they were as anxious to evade the hunters as the hunters were to evade them. Everything that had passed seemed to give evidence of this. The outlaw in the chasm, for instance, could easily have waylaid Rod; a dozen times the almost defenseless camp could have been attacked, and there were innumerable places where ambushes might have been laid for them along the trap-lines.

So Rod's experience with the Woonga trail between the mountains occasioned little uneasiness, and instead of forming a scheme for the further investigation of this trail on the south, plans were made for locating the first fall. Mukoki was the swiftest and most tireless traveler on snow-shoes, and it was he who volunteered to make the first search. He would leave the following morning, taking with him a supply of food, and during his absence Rod and Wabigoon would attend to the traps.

"We must have the location of the first fall before we return to the Post," declared Wabi. "If from that we find that the third fall is not within a hundred miles of our present camp it will be impossible for us to go in search of our gold during this trip. In that event we shall have to go back to Wabinosh House and form a new expedition, with fresh supplies and the proper kind of tools. We can not do anything until the spring freshets are over, anyway."

"I have been thinking of that," replied Rod, his eyes softening. "You know mother is alone, and--her--"

"I understand," interrupted the Indian boy, laying a hand fondly across his companion's arm.

"--her funds are small, you know," Rod finished. "If she has been sick--or--anything like that--"

"Yes, we've got to get back with our furs," helped Wabi, a tremor of tenderness in his own voice. "And if you don't mind, Rod, I might take a little run down to Detroit with you. Do you suppose she would care?"

"Care!" shouted Rod, bringing his free hand down upon Wabi's arm with a force that hurt. "Care! Why, she thinks as much of you as she does of me, Wabi! She'd be tickled to death! Do you mean it?"

Wabi's bronzed face flushed a deeper red at his friend's enthusiasm.

"I won't promise--for sure," he said. "But I'd like to see her--almost as much as you, I guess. If I can, I'll go."

Rod's face was suffused with a joyful glow.

"And I'll come back with you early in the summer and we'll start out for the gold," he cried. He jumped to his feet and slapped Mukoki on the back in the happy turn his mind had taken. "Will you come, too, Mukoki? I'll give you the biggest 'city time' you ever had in your life!"

The old Indian grinned and chuckled and grunted, but did not reply in words. Wabi laughed, and answered for him.

"He is too anxious to become Minnetaki's slave again, Rod. No, Muky won't go, I'll wager that. He will stay at the Post to see that she doesn't get lost, or hurt, or stolen by the Woongas. Eh, Mukoki?" Mukoki nodded, grinning good-humoredly. He went to the door, opened it and looked out.

"Devil--she snow!" he cried. "She snow like twent' t'ousand--like devil!"

This was the strongest English in the old warrior's vocabulary, and it meant something more than usual. Wabi and Rod quickly joined him. Never in his life had the city youth seen a snow-storm like that which he now gazed out into. The great north storm had arrived--a storm which comes just once each year in the endless

Arctic desolation. For days and weeks the Indians had expected it and wondered at its lateness. It fell softly, silently, without a breath of air to stir it; a smothering, voiceless sea of white, impenetrable to human vision, so thick that it seemed as though it might stifle one's breath. Rod held out the palm of his hand and in an instant it was covered with a film of white. He walked out into it, and a dozen yards away he became a ghostly, almost invisible shadow.

When he came back a minute later he brought a load of snow into the cabin with him.

All that afternoon the snow fell like this, and all that night the storm continued. When he awoke in the morning Rod heard the wind whistling and howling through the trees and around the ends of the cabin. He rose and built the fire while the others were still sleeping. He attempted to open the door, but it was blocked. He lowered the barricade at the window, and a barrel of snow tumbled in about his feet. He could see no sign of day, and when he turned he saw Wabi sitting up in his blankets, laughing silently at his wonder and consternation.

"What in the world--" he gasped.

"We're snowed in," grinned Wabi. "Does the stove smoke?"

"No," replied Rod, throwing a bewildered glance at the roaring fire. "You don't mean to say--"

"Then we are not completely, buried," interrupted the other. "At least the top of the chimney is sticking out!"

Mukoki sat up and stretched himself.

"She blow," he said, as a tremendous howl of wind swept over the cabin. "Bime-by she blow some more!"

Rod shoveled the snow into a corner and replaced the barricade while his companions dressed.

"This means a week's work digging out traps," declared Wabi. "And only Mukoki's Great Spirit, who sends all blessings to this country, knows when the blizzard is going to stop. It may last a week. There is no chance of finding our waterfall in this."

"We can play dominoes," suggested Rod cheerfully. "You remember we haven't finished that series we began at the Post. But you don't expect me to believe that it snowed enough yesterday afternoon and last night to cover this cabin, do you?"

"It didn't exactly *snow* enough to cover it," explained his comrade. "But we're covered for all of that. The cabin is on the edge of an open, and of course the snow just naturally drifts around us, blown there by the wind. If this blizzard keeps up we shall be under a small mountain by night."

"Won't it--smother us?" faltered Rod.

Wabi gave a joyous whoop of merriment at the city-bred youth's half-expressed fear and a volley of Mukoki's chuckles came from where he was slicing moose-steak on the table.

"Snow mighty nice thing live under," he asserted with emphasis.

"If you were under a mountain of snow you could live, if you weren't crushed to death," said Wabi. "Snow is filled with air. Mukoki was caught under a snow-slide once and was buried under thirty feet for ten hours. He had made a nest about as big as a barrel and was nice and comfortable when we dug him out. We won't have to burn much wood to keep warm now."

After breakfast the boys again lowered the barricade at the window and Wabi began to bring small avalanches of snow down into the cabin with his shovel. At the third or fourth upward thrust a huge mass plunged through the window, burying them to the waist, and when they looked out they could see the light of day and the whirling blizzard above their heads.

"It's up to the roof," gasped Rod. "Great Scott, what a snow-storm!"

"Now for some fun!" cried the Indian youth. "Come on, Rod, if you want to be in it."

He crawled through the window into the cavity he had made in the drift, and Rod followed. Wabi waited, a mischievous smile on his face, and no sooner had his companion joined him than he plunged his shovel deep into the base of the drift. Half a dozen quick thrusts and there tumbled down upon their heads a mass of light snow that for a few moments completely buried them. The suddenness of it knocked Rod to his knees, where he floundered, gasped and made a vain effort to yell. Struggling like a fish he first kicked his feet free, and Wabi, who had thrust out his head and shoulders, shrieked with laughter as he saw only Rod's boots sticking out of the snow.

"You're going the wrong way, Rod!" he shouted. "Wow--wow!"

He seized his companion's legs and helped to drag him out, and then stood shaking, the tears streaming down his face, and continued to laugh until he leaned back in the drift, half exhausted. Rod was a curious and ludicrous-looking object. His eyes were wide and blinking; the snow was in his ears, his mouth, and in his floundering he had packed his coat collar full of it. Slowly he recovered from his astonishment, saw Wabi and Mukoki quivering with laughter, grinned--and then joined them in their merriment.

It was not difficult now for the boys to force their way through the drift and they were soon standing waist-deep in the snow twenty yards from the cabin.

"The snow is only about four feet deep in the open," said Wabi. "But look at that!"

He turned and gazed at the cabin, or rather at the small part of it which still rose triumphant above the huge drift which had almost completely buried it. Only a little of the roof, with the smoking chimney rising out of it, was to be seen. Rod now turned in all directions to survey the wild scene about him. There had come a brief lull in the blizzard, and his vision extended beyond the lake and to the hilltop. There was not a spot of black to meet his eyes; every rock was hidden; the trees hung silent and lifeless under their heavy mantles and even their trunks were beaten white with the clinging volleys of the storm. There came to him then a thought of the wild things in this seemingly uninhabitable desolation. How could they live in this endless desert of snow? What could they find to eat? Where could they find water to drink? He asked Wabi these questions after they had returned to the cabin.

"Just now, if you traveled from here to the end of this storm zone you wouldn't find a living four-legged creature," said Wabigoon. "Every moose in this country, every deer and caribou, every fox and wolf, is buried in the snow. And as the snow falls deeper about them the warmer and more comfortable do they become, so that even as the blizzard increases in fury the kind Creator makes it easier for them to bear. When the storm ceases the wilderness will awaken into life again. The moose and deer and caribou will rise from their snow-beds and begin to eat the boughs of trees and saplings; a crust will have formed on the snow, and all the smaller animals, like foxes, lynx and wolves, will begin to travel again, and to prey upon others for food. Until they find running water again snow and ice take the place of liquid drink; warm caverns dug in the snow give refuge in place of thick swamp moss and brush and leaves. All the big animals, like moose, deer and caribou, will soon make 'yards' for themselves by trampling down large areas of snow, and in these yards they will gather in big herds, eating their way through the forests, fighting the wolves and waiting for spring. Oh, life isn't altogether bad for the animals in a deep winter like this!"

Until noon the hunters were busy cleaning away the snow from the cabin door. As the day advanced the blizzard increased in its fury, until, with the approach of night, it became impossible for the hunters to expose themselves to it. For three days the storm continued with only intermittent lulls, but with the dawn of the fourth day the sky was again cloudless, and the sun rose with a blinding effulgence. Rod now found himself suffering from that sure affliction of every tenderfoot in the far North--snow-blindness. For only a few minutes at a time could he stand the dazzling reflections of the snow-waste where nothing but white, flashing, scintillating white, seemingly a vast sea of burning electric points in the sunlight, met his aching eyes. On the second day after the storm, while Wabi was still inuring Rod to the changed world and teaching him how to accustom his eyes to it gradually, Mukoki left the cabin to follow the chasm in his search for the first waterfall.

That same day Wabi began his work of digging out and resetting the traps, but it was not until the day following that Rod's eyes would allow him to assist. The task was a most difficult one; rocks and other landmarks were completely hidden, and the lost traps averaged one out of four. It was not until the end of the second day after Mukoki's departure that the young hunters finished the mountain trapline, and when they turned their faces toward camp just at the beginning of dusk it was with the expectant hope that they would find the old Indian awaiting them. But Mukoki had not returned. The next day came and passed, and a fourth dawned without his arrival. Hope now gave way to fear. In three days Mukoki could travel nearly a hundred miles. Was it possible that something had happened to him? Many times there recurred to Rod a thought of the Woonga in the chasm. Had the mysterious spy, or some of his people, waylaid and killed him?

Neither of the hunters had a desire to leave camp during the fourth day. Trapping was exceptionally good now on account of the scarcity of animal food and since the big storm they had captured a wolf, two lynx, a red fox and eight mink. But as Mukoki's absence lengthened their enthusiasm grew less.

In the afternoon, as they were watching, they saw a figure climb wearily to the summit of the hill.

It was Mukoki.

With shouts of greeting both youths hurried through the snow toward him, not taking time to strap on their snow-shoes. The old Indian was at their side a couple of minutes later. He smiled in a tired good-natured way, and answered the eagerness in their eyes with a nod of his head.

"Found fall. Fift' mile down mountain."

Once in the cabin he dropped into a chair, exhausted, and both Rod and Wabigoon joined in relieving him of his boots and outer garments. It was evident that Mukoki had been traveling hard, for only once or twice before in his life had Wabi seen him so completely fatigued. Quickly the young Indian had a huge steak broiling over the fire, and Rod put an extra handful of coffee in the pot.

"Fifty miles!" ejaculated Wabi for the twentieth time. "It was an awful jaunt, wasn't it, Muky?"

"Rough--rough like devil th'ough mountains," replied Mukoki. "Not like that!" He swung an arm in the direction of the chasm.

Rod stood silent, open-eyed with wonder. Was it possible that the old warrior had discovered a wilder country than that through which he had passed in the chasm?

"She little fall," went on Mukoki, brightening as the odor of coffee and meat filled his nostrils. "No bigger than--that!" He pointed to the roof of the cabin.

Rod was figuring on the table. Soon he looked up.

"According to Mukoki and the map we are at least two hundred and fifty miles from the third fall," he said.

Mukoki shrugged his shoulders and his face was crinkled in a suggestive grimace.

"Hudson Bay," he grunted.

Wabi turned from his steak in sudden astonishment.

"Doesn't the chasm continue east?" he almost shouted.

"No. She turn--straight north."

Rod could not understand the change that came over Wabi's face.

"Boys," he said finally, "if that is the case I can tell you where the gold is. If the stream in the chasm turns northward it is bound for just one place--the Albany River, and the Albany River empties into James Bay! The third waterfall, where our treasure in gold is waiting for us, is in the very heart of the wildest and most savage wilderness in North America. It is safe. No other man has ever found it. But to get it means one of the longest and most adventurous expeditions we ever planned in all our lives!"

"Hurrah!" shouted Rod. "Hurrah--"

He had leaped to his feet, forgetful of everything but that their gold was safe, and that their search for it would lead them even to the last fastnesses of the snow-bound and romantic North.

"Next spring, Wabi!" He held out his hand and the two boys joined their pledge in a hearty grip.

"Next spring!" reiterated Wabi.

"And we go in canoe," joined Mukoki. "Creek grow bigger. We make birch-bark canoe at first fall."

"That is better still," added Wabi. "It will be a glorious trip! We'll take a little vacation at the third fall and run up to James Bay."

"James Bay is practically the same as Hudson Bay, isn't it?" asked Rod.

"Yes. I could never see a good reason for calling it James Bay. It is in reality the lower end, or tail, of Hudson Bay."

There was no thought of visiting any of the traps that day, and the next morning Mukoki insisted upon going with Rod, in spite of his four days of hard travel. If he remained in camp his joints would get stiff, he said, and Wabigoon thought he was right. This left the young Indian to care for the trap-line leading into the north.

Two weeks of ideal trapping weather now followed. It had been more than two months since the hunters had left Wabinosh House, and Rod now began to count the days before they would turn back over the homeward trail. Wabi had estimated that they had sixteen hundred dollars' worth of furs and scalps and two hundred dollars in gold, and the white youth was satisfied to return to his mother with his share of six hundred dollars, which was as much as he would have earned in a year at his old position in the city. Neither did he attempt to conceal from Wabi his desire to see Minnetaki; and his Indian friend, thoroughly pleased at Rod's liking for his sister, took much pleasure in frequent good-natured banter on the subject. In fact, Rod possessed a secret hope that he might induce the princess mother to allow her daughter to accompany himself and Wabi to Detroit, where he knew that his own mother would immediately fall in love with the beautiful little maiden from the North.

In the third week after the great storm Rod and Mukoki had gone over the mountain trap-line, leaving Wabi in camp. They had decided that the following week would see them headed for Wabinosh House, where they would arrive about the first of February, and Roderick was in high spirits.

On this day they had started toward camp early in the afternoon, and soon after they had passed through the swamp Rod expressed his intention of ascending the ridge, hoping to get a shot at game somewhere along the mountain trail home. Mukoki, however, decided not to accompany him, but to take the nearer and easier route.

On the top of the mountain Rod paused to take a survey of the country about him. He could see Mukoki, now hardly more than a moving speck on the edge of the plain; northward the same fascinating, never-ending wilderness rolled away under his eyes; eastward, two miles away, he saw a moving object which he knew was a moose or a caribou; and westward--

Instinctively his eyes sought the location of their camp. Instantly the expectant light went out of his face. He gave an involuntary cry of horror, and there followed it a single, unheard shriek for Mukoki.

Over the spot where he knew their camp to be now rose a huge volume of smoke. The sky was black with it, and in the terrible moment that followed his piercing cry for Mukoki he fancied that he heard the sound of rifle-shots.

"Mukoki! Mukoki!" he shouted.

The old Indian was beyond hearing. Quickly it occurred to Rod that early in their trip they had arranged rifle signals for calling help--two quick shots, and then, after a moment's interval, three others in rapid succession.

He threw his rifle to his shoulder and fired into the air; once, twice--and then three times as fast as he could press the trigger.

As he watched Mukoki he reloaded. He saw the Indian pause, turn about and look back toward the mountain.

Again the thrilling signals for help went echoing over the plains. In a few seconds the sounds had reached Mukoki's ears and the old warrior came swinging back at running speed.

Rod darted along the ridge to meet him, firing a single shot now and then to let him know where he was, and in fifteen minutes Mukoki came panting up the mountain.

"The Woongas!" shouted Rod. "They've attacked the camp! See!" He pointed to the cloud of smoke. "I heard shots--I heard shots--"

For an instant the grim pathfinder gazed in the direction of the burning camp, and then without a word he started at terrific speed down the mountain.

The half-hour race that followed was one of the most exciting experiences of Rod's life. How he kept up with Mukoki was more than he ever could explain afterward. But from the time they struck the old trail he was close at the Indian's heels. When they reached the hill that sheltered the dip his face was scratched and bleeding from contact with swinging bushes; his heart seemed ready to burst from its tremendous exertion; his breath came in an audible hissing, rattling sound, and he could not speak. But up the hill he plunged behind Mukoki, his rifle cocked and ready. At the top they paused.

The camp was a smoldering mass of ruins. Not a sign of life was about it. But--

With a gasping, wordless cry Rod caught Mukoki's arm and pointed to an object lying in the snow a dozen yards from where the cabin had been. The warrior had seen it. He turned one look upon the white youth, and it was a look that Rod had never thought could come into the face of a human being. If that was Wabi down there--if Wabi had been killed--what would Mukoki's vengeance be! His companion was no longer Mukoki--as he had known him; he was the savage. There was no mercy, no human instinct, no suggestion of the human soul in that one terrible look. If it was Wabi--

They plunged down the hill, into the dip, across the lake, and Mukoki was on his knees beside the figure in the snow. He turned it over--and rose without a sound, his battle-glaring eyes peering into the smoking ruins.

Rod looked, and shuddered.

The figure in the snow was not Wabi.

It was a strange, terrible-looking object--a giant Indian, distorted in death--and a half of his head was shot away!

When he again looked at Mukoki the old Indian was in the midst of the hot ruins, kicking about with his booted feet and poking with the butt of his rifle.

CHAPTER XIV
THE RESCUE OF WABIGOON

Rod had sunk into the snow close to the dead man. His endurance was gone and he was as weak as a child. He watched every movement Mukoki made; saw every start, every glance, and became almost sick with fear whenever the warrior bent down to examine some object.

Was Wabi dead--and burned in those ruins?

Foot by foot Mukoki searched. His feet became hot; the smell of burning leather filled his nostrils; glowing coals burned through to his feet. But the old Indian was beyond pain. Only two things filled his soul. One of these was love for Minnetaki; the other was love for Wabigoon. And there was only one other thing that could take the place of these, and that was merciless, undying, savage passion--passion at any wrong or injury that might be done to them. The Woongas had sneaked upon Wabi. He knew that. They had caught him unaware, like cowards; and perhaps he was dead--and in those ruins!

He searched until his feet were scorched and burned in a score of places, and then he came out, smoke-blackened, but with some of the terrible look gone out of his face.

"He no there!" he said, speaking for the first time.

Again he crouched beside the dead man, and grimaced at Rod with a triumphant, gloating chuckle.

"Much dead!" he grinned.

In a moment the grimace had gone from his face, and while Rod still rested he continued his examination of the camp. Close around it the snow was beaten down with human tracks. Mukoki saw where the outlaws had stolen up behind the cabin from the forest and he saw where they had gone away after the attack.

The Wolf Hunters

Five had come down from the cedars, only four had gone away!

Where was Wabi?

If he had been captured, and taken with the Indians, there would have been five trails. Rod understood this as well as Mukoki, and he also understood why his companion went back to make another investigation of the smoldering ruins. This second search, however, convinced the Indian that Wabi's body had not been thrown into the fire. There was only one conclusion to draw. The youth had made a desperate fight, had killed one of the outlaws, and after being wounded in the conflict had been carried off bodily. Wabi and his captors could not be more than two or three miles away. A quick pursuit would probably overtake them within an hour.

Mukoki came to Rod's side.

"Me follow--kill!" he said. "Me kill so many quick!" He pointed toward the four trails. "You stay--"

Rod clambered to his feet.

"You mean we'll kill 'em, Muky," he broke in. "I can follow you again. Set the pace!"

There came the click of the safety on Mukoki's rifle, and Rod, following suit, cocked his own.

"Much quiet," whispered the Indian when they had come to the farther side of the dip. "No noise--come up still--shoot!"

The snow-shoe trail of the outlaws turned from the dip into the timbered bottoms to the north, and Mukoki, partly crouched, his rifle always to the front, followed swiftly. They had not progressed a hundred yards into the plain when the old hunter stopped, a puzzled look in his face. He pointed to one of the snow-shoe trails which was much deeper than the others.

"Heem carry Wabi," he spoke softly. "But--" His eyes gleamed in sudden excitement. "They go slow! They no hurry! Walk very slow! Take much time!"

Rod now observed for the first time that the individual tracks made by the outlaws were much shorter than their own, showing that instead of being in haste they were traveling quite slowly. This was a mystery which was not easy to explain. Did the Woongas not fear pursuit? Was it possible that they believed the hunters would not hasten to give them battle? Or were they relying upon the strength of their numbers, or, perhaps, planning some kind of ambush?

Mukoki's advance now became slower and more cautious. His keen eyes took in every tree and clump of bushes ahead. Only when he could see the trail leading straight away for a considerable distance did he hasten the pursuit. Never for an instant did he turn his head to Rod. But suddenly he caught sight of something that brought from him a guttural sound of astonishment. A fifth track had joined the trail! Without questioning Rod knew what it meant. Wabi had been lowered from the back of his captor and was now walking. He was on snow-shoes and his strides were quite even and of equal length with the others. Evidently he was not badly wounded.

Half a mile ahead of them was a high hill and between them and this hill was a dense growth of cedar, filled with tangled windfalls. It was an ideal place for an ambush, but the old warrior did not hesitate. The Woongas had followed a moose trail, with which they were apparently well acquainted, and in this traveling was easy. But Rod gave an involuntary shudder as he gazed ahead into the chaotic tangle through which it led. At any moment he expected to hear the sharp crack of a rifle and to see Mukoki tumble forward upon his face. Or there might be a fusillade of shots and he himself might feel the burning sting that comes with rifle death. At the distance from which they would shoot the outlaws could not miss. Did not Mukoki realize this? Maddened by the thought that his beloved Wabi was in the hands of merciless enemies, was the old pathfinder becoming reckless?

But when he looked into his companion's face and saw the cool deadly resolution glittering in his eyes, the youth's confidence was restored. For some reason Mukoki knew that there would not be an ambush.

Over the moose-run the two traveled more swiftly and soon they came to the foot of the high hill. Up this the Woongas had gone, their trail clearly defined and unswerving in its direction. Mukoki now paused with a warning gesture to Rod, and pointed down at one of the snow-shoe tracks. The snow was still crumbling and falling about the edges of this imprint.

"Ver' close!" whispered the Indian.

It was not the light of the game hunt in Mukoki's eyes now; there was a trembling, terrible tenseness in his whispered words. He crept up the hill with Rod so near that he could have touched him. At the summit of that hill he dragged himself up like an animal, and then, crouching, ran swiftly to the opposite side, his rifle within six inches of his shoulder. In the plain below them was unfolded to their eyes a scene which, despite his companion's warning, wrung an exclamation of dismay from Roderick's lips.

Plainly visible to them in the edge of the plain were the outlaw Woongas and their captive. They were in single file, with Wabi following the leader, and the hunters perceived that their comrade's arms were tied behind him.

But it was another sight that caused Rod's dismay.

From an opening beside a small lake half a mile beyond the Indians below there rose the smoke of two camp-fires, and Mukoki and he could make out at least a score of figures about these fires.

Within rifle-shot of them, almost within shouting distance, there was not only the small war party that had attacked the camp, but a third of the fighting men of the Woonga tribe! Rod understood their terrible predicament. To attack the outlaws in an effort to rescue Wabi meant that an overwhelming force would be upon them within a few minutes; to allow Wabi to remain a captive meant--he shuddered at the thought of what it might mean, for he knew of the merciless vengeance of the Woongas upon the House of Wabinosh.

And while he was thinking of these things the faithful old warrior beside him had already formed his plan of attack. He would die with Wabi, gladly--a fighting, terrible slave to devotion to the last; but he would not see Wabi die alone. A whispered word, a last look at his rifle, and Mukoki hurried down into the plains.

At the foot of the hill he abandoned the outlaw trail and Rod realized that his plan was to sweep swiftly in a semicircle, surprising the Woongas from the front or side instead of approaching from the rear. Again he was taxed to his utmost to keep pace with the avenging Mukoki. Less than ten minutes later the Indian peered cautiously from behind a clump of hazel, and then looked back at Rod, a smile of satisfaction on his face.

"They come," he breathed, just loud enough to hear. "They come!"

Rod peered over his shoulder, and his heart smote mightily within him. Unconscious of their peril the Woongas were approaching two hundred yards away. Mukoki gazed into his companion's face and his eyes were almost pleading as he laid a bronzed crinkled hand upon the white boy's arm.

"You take front man--ahead of Wabi," he whispered. "I take other t'ree. See that tree--heem birch, with bark off? Shoot heem there. You no tremble? You no miss?"

"No," replied Rod. He gripped the red hand in his own. "I'll kill, Mukoki. I'll kill him dead--in one shot!"

They could hear the voices of the outlaws now, and soon they saw that Wabi's face was disfigured with blood.

Step by step, slowly and carelessly, the Woongas approached. They were fifty yards from the marked birch now--forty--thirty--now only ten. Roderick's rifle was at his shoulder. Already it held a deadly bead on the breast of the leader.

Five yards more--

The outlaw passed behind the tree; he came out, and the young hunter pressed the trigger. The leader stopped in his snow-shoes. Even before he had crumpled down into a lifeless heap in the snow a furious volley of shots spat forth from Mukoki's gun, and when Rod swung his own rifle to join again in the fray he found that only one of the four was standing, and he with his hands to his breast as he tottered about to fall. But from some one of those who had fallen there had gone out a wild, terrible cry, and even as Rod and Makoki rushed out to free Wabigoon there came an answering yell from the direction of the Woonga camp.

Mukoki's knife was in his hand by the time he reached Wabi, and with one or two slashes he had released his hands.

"You hurt--bad?" he asked.

"No--no!" replied Wabi. "I knew you'd come, boys--dear old friends!"

As he spoke he turned to the fallen leader and Rod saw him take possession of the rifle and revolver which he had lost in their fight with the Woongas weeks before. Mukoki had already spied their precious pack of furs on one of the outlaw's backs, and he flung it over his own.

"You saw the camp?" queried Wabi excitedly.

"Yes."

"They will be upon us in a minute! Which way, Mukoki?"

"The chasm!" half shouted Rod. "The chasm! If we can reach the chasm--"

"The chasm!" reiterated Wabigoon.

Mukoki had fallen behind and motioned for Wabi and Rod to take the lead.

Even now he was determined to take the brunt of danger by bringing up the rear.

There was no time for argument and Wabigoon set off at a rapid pace. From behind there came the click of shells as the Indian loaded his rifle on the run. While the other two had been busy at the scene of the ambush Rod had replaced his empty shell, and now, as he led, Wabi examined the armament that had been stolen from them by the outlaws.

"How many shells have you got, Rod?" he asked over his shoulder.

"Forty-nine."

"There's only four left in this belt besides five in the gun," called back the Indian youth. "Give me--some."

Without halting Rod plucked a dozen cartridges from his belt and passed them on.

Now they had reached the hill. At its summit they paused to recover their breath and take a look at the camp.

The fires were deserted. A quarter of a mile out on the plain they saw half a dozen of their pursuers speeding toward the hill. The rest were already concealed in the nearer thickets of the bottom.

"We must beat them to the chasm!" said the young Indian.

As he spoke Wabi turned and led the way again.

Rod's heart fell like a lump within him. We must beat them to the chasm! Those words of Wabi's brought him to the terrible realization that his own powers of endurance were rapidly ebbing. His race behind Mukoki to the burning cabin had seemed to rob the life from the muscles of his limbs, and each step now added to his weakness. And the chasm was a mile beyond the dip, and the entrance into that chasm still two miles farther. Three miles! Could he hold out?

He heard Mukoki thumping along behind him; ahead of him Wabi was unconsciously widening the distance between them. He made a powerful effort to close the breach, but it was futile. Then from close in his rear there came a warning halloo from the old Indian, and Wabi turned.

"He run t'ree mile to burning cabin," said Mukoki. "He no make chasm!"

Rod was deathly white and breathing so hard that he could not speak. The quick-witted Wabi at once realized their situation.

"There is just one thing for us to do, Muky. We must stop the Woongas at the dip. We'll fire down upon them from the top of the hill beyond the lake. We can drop three or four of them and they won't dare to come straight after us then. They will think we are going to fight them from there and will take time to sneak around us. Meanwhile we'll get a good lead in the direction of the chasm."

He led off again, this time a little slower. Three minutes later they entered into the dip, crossed it safely, and were already at the foot of the hill, when from the opposite side of the hollow there came a triumphant blood-curdling yell.

"Hurry!" shouted Wabi. "They see us!" Even as he spoke there came the crack of a rifle.

Bzzzzzzz-inggggg!

For the first time in his life Rod heard that terrible death-song of a bullet close to his head and saw the snow fly up a dozen feet beyond the young Indian.

For an interval of twenty seconds there was silence; then there came another shot, and after that three others in quick succession. Wabi stumbled.

"Not hit!" he called, scrambling to his feet. "Confound--that rock!"

He rose to the hilltop with Rod close behind him, and from the opposite side of the lake there came a fusillade of half a dozen shots. Instinctively Rod dropped upon his face. And in that instant, as he lay in the snow, he heard the sickening thud of a bullet and a sharp sudden cry of pain from Mukoki. But the old warrior came up beside him and they passed into the shelter of the hilltop together.

"Is it bad? Is it bad, Mukoki? Is it bad--" Wabi was almost sobbing as he turned and threw an arm around the old Indian. "Are you hit--bad?"

Mukoki staggered, but caught himself.

"In here," he said, putting a hand to his left shoulder. "She--no--bad." He smiled, courage gleaming with pain in his eyes, and swung off the light pack of furs. "We give 'em--devil--here!"

Crouching, they peered over the edge of the hill. Half a dozen Woongas had already left the cedars and were following swiftly across the open. Others broke from the cover, and Wabi saw that a number of them were without snow-shoes. He exultantly drew Mukoki's attention to this fact, but the latter did not lift his eyes. In a few moments he spoke.

"Now we give 'em--devil!"

Eight pursuers on snow-shoes were in the open of the dip. Six of them had reached the lake. Rod held his fire. He knew that it was now more important for him to recover his wind than to fight, and he drew great drafts of air into his lungs while his two comrades leveled their rifles. He could fire after they were done if it was necessary.

There was slow deadly deliberation in the way Mukoki and Wabigoon sighted along their rifle-barrels. Mukoki fired first; one shot, two--with a second's interval between--and an outlaw half-way across the lake pitched forward into the snow. As he fell, Wabi fired once, and there came to their ears shriek after shriek of agony as a second pursuer fell with a shattered leg. At the cries and shots of battle the hot blood rushed through Rod's veins, and with an excited shout of defiance he brought his rifle to his shoulder and in unison the three guns sent fire and death into the dip below.

Only three of the eight Woongas remained and they had turned and were running toward the shelter of the cedars.

"Hurrah!" shouted Rod.

In his excitement he got upon his feet and sent his fifth and last shot after the fleeing outlaws. "Hurrah! Wow! Let's go after 'em!"

"Get down!" commanded Wabi. "Load in a hurry!"

Clink--clink--clink sounded the new shells as Mukoki and Wabigoon thrust them into their magazines. Five seconds more and they were sending a terrific fusillade of shots into the edge of the cedars--ten in all--and by the time he had reloaded his own gun Rod could see nothing to shoot at.

"That will hold them for a while," spoke Wabi. "Most of them came in too big a hurry, and without their snow-shoes, Muky. We'll beat them to the chasm--easy!" He put an arm around the shoulders of the old Indian, who was still lying upon his face in the snow. "Let me see, Muky--let me see--"

"Chasm first," replied Mukoki. "She no bad. No hit bone. No bleed--much."

From behind Rod could see that Mukoki's coat was showing a growing blotch of red.

"Are you sure--you can reach the chasm?"

"Yes."

In proof of his assertion the wounded Indian rose to his feet and approached the pack of furs. Wabi was ahead of him, and placed it upon his own shoulders.

"You and Rod lead the way," he said. "You two know where to find the opening into the chasm. I've never been there."

Mukoki started down the hill, and Rod, close behind, could hear him breathing heavily; there was no longer fear for himself in his soul, but for that grim faithful warrior ahead, who would die in his tracks without a murmur and with a smile of triumph and fearlessness on his lips.

CHAPTER XV
RODERICK HOLDS THE WOONGAS AT BAY

They traveled more slowly now and Rod found his strength returning. When they reached the second ridge he took Mukoki by the arm and assisted him up, and the old Indian made no demur. This spoke more strongly of his hurt than words. There was still no sign of their enemies behind. From the top of the second ridge they could look back upon a quarter of a mile of the valley below, and it was here that Rod suggested that he remain on watch for a few minutes while Wabigoon went on with Mukoki. The young hunters could see that the Indian was becoming weaker at every step, and Mukoki could no longer conceal this weakness in spite of the tremendous efforts he made to appear natural.

"I believe it is bad," whispered Wabi to Rod, his face strangely white. "I believe it is worse than we think. He is bleeding hard. Your idea is a good one. Watch here, and if the Woongas show up in the valley open fire on them. I'll leave you my gun, too, so they'll think we are going to give them another fight. That will keep them back for a time. I'm going to stop Muky up here a little way and dress his wound. He will bleed to death if I don't."

"And then go on," added Rod. "Don't stop if you hear me fire, but hurry on to the chasm. I know the way and will join you. I'm as strong as I ever was now, and can catch up with you easily with Mukoki traveling as slowly as he does."

During this brief conversation Mukoki had continued his way along the ridge and Wabi hurried to overtake him. Meanwhile Rod concealed himself behind a rock, from which vantage-point he could see the whole of that part of the valley across which they had come.

He looked at his watch and in tense anxiety counted every minute after that. He allowed ten minutes for the dressing of Mukoki's wound. Every second gained from then on would be priceless. For a quarter of an hour he kept his eyes with ceaseless vigilance upon their back trail. Surely the Woongas had secured their snow-shoes by this time! Was it possible that they had given up the pursuit--that their terrible experience in the dip had made them afraid of further battle? Rod answered this question in the negative. He was sure that the Woongas knew that Wabi was the son of the factor of Wabinosh House. Therefore they would make every effort to recapture him, even though they had to follow far and a dozen lives were lost before that feat was accomplished.

A movement in the snow across the valley caught Rod's eyes. He straightened himself, and his breath came quickly. Two figures had appeared in the open. Another followed close behind, and after that there came others, until the waiting youth had counted sixteen. They were all on snow-shoes, following swiftly over the trail of the fugitives.

The young hunter looked at his watch again. Twenty-five minutes had passed. Mukoki and Wabigoon had secured a good start. If he could only hold the outlaws in the valley for a quarter of an hour more--just fifteen short minutes--they would almost have reached the entrance into the chasm.

Alone, with his own life and those of his comrades depending upon him, the boy was cool. There was no tremble in his hands to destroy the accuracy of his rifle-fire, no blurring excitement or fear in his brain to trouble his judgment of distance and range. He made up his mind that he would not fire until they had come within four hundred yards. Between that distance and three hundred he was sure he could drop at least one or two of them.

He measured his range by a jackpine stub, and when two of the Woongas had reached and passed that stub he fired. He saw the snow thrown up six feet in front of the leader. He fired again, and again, and one of the shots, a little high, struck the second outlaw. The leader had darted back to the shelter of the stub and Rod sent another bullet whizzing past his ears. His fifth he turned into the main body of the pursuers, and then, catching up Wabi's rifle, he poured a hail of five bullets among them in as many seconds.

The effect was instantaneous. The outlaws scattered in retreat and Rod saw that a second figure was lying motionless in the snow. He began to reload his rifles and by the time he had finished the Woongas had separated and were running to the right and the left of him. For the last time he looked at his watch. Wabi and Mukoki had been gone thirty-five minutes.

The boy crept back from his rock, straightened himself, and followed in their trail. He mentally calculated that it would be ten minutes before the Woongas, coming up from the sides and rear, would discover his flight, and by that time he would have nearly a mile the start of them. He saw, without stopping, where Wabi had dressed Mukoki's wound. There were spots of blood and a red rag upon the snow. Half a mile farther on the two had paused again, and this time he knew that Mukoki had stopped to rest. From now on they had rested every quarter of a mile or so, and soon Roderick saw them toiling slowly through the snow ahead of him.

He ran up, panting, anxious.

"How--" he began.

Wabi looked at him grimly.

"How much farther, Rod?" he asked.

"Not more than half a mile."

Wabi motioned for him to take Mukoki's other arm.

"He has bled a good deal," he said. There was a hardness in his voice that made Rod shudder, and he caught his breath as Wabi shot him a meaning glance behind the old warrior's doubled shoulders.

They went faster now, almost carrying their wounded comrade between them. Suddenly, Wabi paused, threw his rifle to his shoulder, and fired. A few yards ahead a huge white rabbit kicked in his death struggles in the snow.

"If we do reach the chasm Mukoki must have something to eat," he said.

"We'll reach it!" gasped Rod. "We'll reach it! There's the woods. We go down there!"

They almost ran, with Mukoki's snow-shod feet dragging between them, and five minutes later they were carrying the half-unconscious Indian down the steep side of the mountain. At its foot Wabi turned, and his eyes flashed with vengeful hatred.

"Now, you devils!" he shouted up defiantly. "Now!"

Mukoki aroused himself for a few moments and Rod helped him back to the shelter of the chasm wall. He found a nook between great masses of rock, almost clear of snow, and left him there while he hurried back to Wabigoon.

"You stand on guard here, Rod," said the latter. "We must cook that rabbit and get some life back into Mukoki. I think he has stopped bleeding, but I am going to look again. The wound isn't fatal, but it has weakened him. If we can get something hot into him I believe he will be able to walk again. Did you have anything left over from your dinner on the trail to-day?"

Rod unstrapped the small pack in which the hunters carried their food while on the trail, and which had been upon his shoulders since noon.

"There is a double handful of coffee, a cupful of tea, plenty of salt and a little bread," he said.

"Good! Few enough supplies for three people in this kind of a wilderness--but they'll save Mukoki!"

Wabi went back, while Rod, sheltered behind a rock, watched the narrow incline into the chasm. He almost hoped the Woongas would dare to attempt a descent, for he was sure that he and Wabi would have them at a terrible disadvantage and with their revolvers and three rifles could inflict a decisive blow upon them before they reached the bottom. But he saw no sign of their enemies. He heard no sound from above, yet he knew that the outlaws were very near--only waiting for the protecting darkness of night.

He heard the crackling of Wabi's fire and the odor of coffee came to him; and Wabi, assured that their presence was known to the Woongas, began whistling cheerily. In a few minutes he rejoined Rod behind the rock.

"They will attack us as soon as it gets good and dark," he said coolly. "That is, if they can find us. As soon as they are no longer able to see down into the chasm we will find some kind of a hiding-place. Mukoki will be able to travel then."

A memory of the cleft in the chasm wall came to Rod and he quickly described it to his companion. It was an ideal hiding-place at night, and if Mukoki was strong enough they could steal up out of the chasm and secure a long start into the south before the Woongas discovered their flight in the morning. There was just one chance of failure. If the spy whose trail had revealed the break in the mountain to Rod was not among the outlaws' wounded or dead the cleft might be guarded, or the Woongas themselves might employ it in making a descent upon them.

"It's worth the risk anyway," said Wabi. "The chances are even that your outlaw ran across the fissure by accident and that his companions are not aware of its existence. And they'll not follow our trail down the chasm to-night, I'll wager. In the cover of darkness they will steal down among the rocks and then wait for daylight. Meanwhile we can be traveling southward and when they catch up with us we will give them another fight if they want it."

"We can start pretty soon?"

"Within an hour."

For some time the two stood in silent watchfulness. Suddenly Rod asked:

"Where is Wolf?"

Wabi laughed, softly, exultantly.

"Gone back to his people, Rod. He will be crying in the wild hunt-pack to-night. Good old Wolf!" The laugh left his lips and there was a tremble of regret in his voice. "The Woongas came from the back of the cabin--took me by surprise--and we had it hot and heavy for a few minutes. We fell back where Wolf was tied and just as I knew they'd got me sure I cut his babeesh with the knife I had in my hand."

"Didn't he show fight?"

"For a minute. Then one of the Indians shot, at him and he hiked off into the woods."

"Queer they didn't wait for Mukoki and me," mused Rod. "Why didn't they ambush us?"

"Because they didn't want you, and they were sure they'd reach their camp before you took up the trail. I was their prize. With me in their power they figured on communicating with you and Mukoki and sending you back to the Post with their terms. They would have bled father to his last cent--and then killed me. Oh, they talked pretty plainly to me when they thought they had me!"

There came a noise from above them and the young hunters held their rifles in readiness. Nearer and nearer came the crashing sound, until a small boulder shot past them into the chasm.

"They're up there," grinned Wabi, lowering his gun. "That was an accident, but you'd better keep your eyes open. I'll bet the whole tribe feel like murdering the fellow who rolled over that stone!"

He crept cautiously back to Mukoki, and Rod crouched with his face to the narrow trail leading down from the top of the mountain. Deep shadows were beginning to lurk among the trees and he was determined that any movement there would draw his fire. Fifteen minutes later Wabi returned, eating ravenously at a big hind quarter of broiled rabbit.

"I've had my coffee," he greeted. "Go back and eat and drink, and build the fire up high. Don't mind me when I shoot. I am going to fire just to let the Woongas know we are on guard, and after that we'll hustle for that break in the mountain."

Rod found Mukoki with a chunk of rabbit in one hand and a cup of coffee in the other. The wounded Indian smiled with something like the old light in his eyes and a mighty load was lifted from Rod's heart.

"You're better?" he asked.

"Fine!" replied Mukoki. "No much hurt. Good fight some more. Wabi say, 'No, you stay.'" His face became a map of grimaces to show his disapproval of Wabi's command.

Rod helped himself to the meat and coffee. He was hungry, but after he was done there remained some of the rabbit and a biscuit and these he placed in his pack for further use. Soon after this there came two shots from the rock and before the echoes had died away down the chasm Wabi approached through the gathering gloom.

It was easy for the hunters to steal along the concealment of the mountain wall, and even if there had been prying eyes on the opposite ridge they could not have penetrated the thickening darkness in the bottom of the gulch. For some time the flight was continued with extreme caution, no sound being made to arouse the suspicion of any outlaw who might be patrolling the edge of the precipice. At the end of half an hour Mukoki, who was in the lead that he might set a pace according to his strength, quickened his steps. Rod was close beside him now, his eyes ceaselessly searching the chasm wall for signs that would tell him when they were nearing the rift. Suddenly Wabi halted in his tracks and gave a low hiss that stopped them.

"It's snowing!" he whispered.

Mukoki lifted his face. Great solitary flakes of snow fell upon it.

"She snow hard--soon. Mebby cover snow-shoe trails!"

"And if it does--we're safe!" There was a vibrant joy in Wabi's voice.

For a full minute Mukoki held his face to the sky.

"Hear small wind over chasm," he said.

"She come from south. She snow hard--now--up there!"

They went on, stirred by new hope. Rod could feel that the flakes were coming thicker. The three now kept close to the chasm wall in their search for the rift. How changed all things were at night! Rod's heart throbbed now with hope, now with doubt, now with actual fear. Was it possible that he could not find it? Had they passed it among some of the black shadows behind? He saw no rock that he recognized, no overhanging crag, no sign to guide him. He stopped, and his voice betrayed his uneasiness as he asked:

"How far do you think we have come?"

Mukoki had gone a few steps ahead, and before Wabi answered he called softly to them from close up against the chasm wall. They hurried to him and found him standing beside the rift.

"Here!"

Wabi handed his rifle to Rod.

"I'm going up first," he announced. "If the coast is clear I'll whistle down."

For a few moments Mukoki and Rod could hear him as he crawled up the fissure. Then all was silent. A quarter of an hour passed, and a low whistle came to their ears. Another ten minutes and the three stood together at the top of the mountain, Rod and the wounded Mukoki breathing hard from their exertions.

For a time the three sat down in the snow and waited, watched, listened; and from Rod's heart there went up something that was almost a prayer, for it was snowing--snowing hard, and it seemed to him that the storm was something which God had specially directed should fall in their path that it might shield them and bring them safely home.

And when he rose to his feet Wabi was still silent, and the three gripped hands in mute thankfulness at their deliverance.

Still speechless, they turned instinctively for a moment back to the dark desolation beyond the chasm--the great, white wilderness in which they had passed so many adventurous yet happy weeks; and as they gazed into the chaos beyond the second mountain there came to them the lonely, wailing howl of a wolf.

"I wonder," said Wabi softly. "I wonder--if that--is Wolf?"

And then, Indian file, they trailed into the south.

CHAPTER XVI
THE SURPRISE AT THE POST

From the moment that the adventurers turned their backs upon the Woonga country Mukoki was in command. With the storm in their favor everything else now depended upon the craft of the old pathfinder. There was neither moon nor wind to guide them, and even Wabi felt that he was not competent to strike a straight trail in a strange country and a night storm. But Mukoki, still a savage in the ways of the wilderness, seemed possessed of that mysterious sixth sense which is known as the sense of orientation--that almost supernatural instinct which guides the carrier pigeon as straight as a die to its home-cote hundreds of miles away. Again and again during that thrilling night's flight Wabi or Rod would ask the Indian where Wabinosh House lay, and he would point out its direction to them without hesitation. And each time it seemed to the city youth that he pointed a different way, and it proved to him how easy it was to become hopelessly lost in the wilderness.

Not until midnight did they pause to rest. They had traveled slowly but steadily and Wabi figured that they had covered fifteen miles. Five miles behind them their trail was completely obliterated by the falling snow. Morning would betray to the Woongas no sign of the direction taken by the fugitives.

"They will believe that we have struck directly westward for the Post," said Wabi. "To-morrow night we'll be fifty miles apart."

During this stop a small fire was built behind a fallen log and the hunters refreshed themselves with a pot of strong coffee and what little remained of the rabbit and biscuits. The march was then resumed.

It seemed to Rod that they had climbed an interminable number of ridges and had picked their way through an interminable number of swampy bottoms between them, and he, even more than Mukoki, was relieved when they struck the easier traveling of open plains. In fact, Mukoki seemed scarcely to give a thought to his wound and Roderick was almost ready to drop in his tracks by the time a halt was called an hour before dawn. The old warrior was confident that they were now well out of danger and a rousing camp-fire was built in the shelter of a thick growth of spruce.

"Spruce partridge in mornin'," affirmed Mukoki. "Plenty here for breakfast."

"How do you know?" asked Rod, whose hunger was ravenous.

"Fine thick spruce, all in shelter of dip," explained the Indian. "Birds winter here."

Wabi had unpacked the furs, and the larger of these, including six lynx and three especially fine wolf skins, he divided into three piles.

"They'll make mighty comfortable beds if you keep close enough to the fire," he explained. "Get a few spruce boughs, Rod, and cover them over with one of the wolf skins. The two lynx pelts will make the warmest blankets you ever had."

Rod quickly availed himself of this idea, and within half an hour he was sleeping soundly. Mukoki and Wabigoon, more inured to the hardships of the wilderness, took only brief snatches of slumber, one or both awakening now and then to replenish the fire. As soon as it was light enough the two Indians went quietly out into the spruce with their guns, and their shots a little later awakened Rod. When they returned they brought three partridges with them.

"There are dozens of them among the spruce," said Wabi, "but just now we do not want to shoot any oftener than is absolutely necessary. Have you noticed our last night's trail?"

Rod rubbed his eyes, thus confessing that as yet he had not been out from between his furs.

"Well, if you go out there in the open for a hundred yards you won't find it," finished his comrade. "The snow has covered it completely."

Although they lacked everything but meat, this breakfast in the spruce thicket was one of the happiest of the entire trip, and when the three hunters were done each had eaten of his partridge until only the bones were left. There was now little cause for fear, for it was still snowing and their enemies were twenty-five miles to the north of them. This fact did not deter the adventurers from securing an early start, however, and they traveled southward through the storm until noon, when they built a camp of spruce and made preparations to rest until the following day.

"We must be somewhere near the Kenogami trail," Wabi remarked to Mukoki. "We may have passed it."

"No pass it," replied Mukoki. "She off there." He pointed to the south.

"You see the Kenogami trail is a sled trail leading from the little town of Nipigon, on the railroad, to Kenogami House, which is a Hudson Bay Post at the upper end of Long Lake," explained Wabi to his white companion. "The factor of Kenogami is a great friend of ours and we have visited back and forth often, but I've been over the Kenogami trail only once. Mukoki has traveled it many times."

Several rabbits were killed before dinner. No other hunting was done during the afternoon, most of which was passed in sleep by the exhausted adventurers. When Rod awoke he found that it had stopped snowing and was nearly dark.

Mukoki's wound was beginning to trouble him again, and it was decided that at least a part of the next day should be passed in camp, and that both Rod and Wabigoon should make an effort to kill some animal that would furnish them with the proper kind of oil to dress it with, the fat of almost any species of animal except mink or rabbit being valuable for this purpose. With dawn the two started out, while Mukoki, much against his will, was induced to remain in camp. A short distance away the hunters separated, Rod striking to the eastward and Wabi into the south.

For an hour Roderick continued without seeing game, though there were plenty of signs of deer and caribou about him. At last he determined to strike for a ridge a mile to the south, from the top of which he was more likely to get a shot than in the thick growth of the plains. He had not traversed more than a half of the distance when much to his surprise he came upon a well-beaten trail running slightly diagonally with his own, almost due north. Two dog-teams had passed since yesterday's storm, and on either side of the sleds were the snow-shoe trails of men. Rod saw that there were three of these, and at least a dozen dogs in the two teams. It at once occurred to him that this was the Kenogami trail, and impelled by nothing more than curiosity he began to follow it.

Half a mile farther on he found where the party had stopped to cook a meal. The remains of their camp-fire lay beside a huge log, which was partly burned away, and about it were scattered bones and bits of bread. But what most attracted Rod's attention were other tracks which joined those of the three people on snow-shoes. He was sure that these tracks had been made by women, for the footprints made by one of them were unusually small. Close to the log he found a single impression in the snow that caused his heart to give a sudden unexpected thump within him. In this spot the snow had been packed by one of the snow-shoes, and in this comparatively hard surface the footprint was clearly defined. It had been made by a moccasin. Rod knew that. And the moccasin wore a slight heel! He remembered, now, that thrilling day in the forest near Wabinosh House when he had stopped to look at Minnetaki's footprints in the soft earth through which she had been driven by her Woonga abductors, and he remembered, too, that she was the only person at the Post who wore heels on her moccasins. It was a queer coincidence! Could Minnetaki have been here? Had she made that footprint in the snow? Impossible, declared the young hunter's better sense. And yet his blood ran a little faster as he touched the delicate impression with his bare fingers. It reminded him of Minnetaki, anyway; her foot would have made just such a trail, and he wondered if the girl who had stepped there was as pretty as she.

He followed now a little faster than before, and ten minutes later he came to where a dozen snow-shoe trails had come in from the north and had joined the three. After meeting, the two parties had evidently joined forces and had departed over the trail made by those who had appeared from the direction of the Post.

"Friends from Kenogami House came down to meet them," mused Rod, and as he turned back in the direction of the camp he formed a picture of that meeting in the heart of the wilderness, of the glad embraces of husband and wife, and the joy of the pretty girl with the tiny feet as she kissed her father, and perhaps her big brother; for no girl could possess feet just like Minnetaki's and not be pretty!

He found that Wabi had preceded him when he returned. The young Indian had shot a small doe, and that noon witnessed a feast in camp. For his lack of luck Rod had his story to tell of the people on the trail. The passing of this party formed the chief topic of conversation during the rest of the day, for after weeks of isolation in the wilderness even this momentary nearness of living civilized men and women was a great event to them. But there was one fact which Rod dwelt but slightly upon. He did not emphasize the similarity of the pretty footprint and that made by

Minnetaki's moccasin, for he knew that a betrayal of his knowledge and admiration of the Indian maiden's feet would furnish Wabi with fun-making ammunition for a week. He did say, however, that the footprint in the snow struck him as being just about the size that Minnetaki would make.

All that day and night the hunters remained in camp, sleeping, eating and taking care of Mukoki's wound, but the next morning saw them ready for their homeward journey with the coming of dawn. They struck due westward now, satisfied that they were well beyond the range of the outlaw Woongas.

As the boys talked over their adventure on the long journey back toward the Post, Wabi thought with regret of the moose head which he had left buried in the "Indian ice-box," and even wished, for a moment, to go home by the northern trail, despite the danger from the hostile Woongas, in order to recover the valuable antlers. But Mukoki shook his head.

"Woonga make good fight. What for go again into wolf trap?"

And so they reluctantly gave up the notion of carrying the big head of the bull moose back to the Post.

A little before noon of the second day they saw Lake Nipigon from the top of a hill. Columbus when he first stepped upon the shore of his newly discovered land was not a whit happier than Roderick Drew when that joyous youth, running out upon the snow-covered ice, attempted to turn a somersault with his snow-shoes on!

Just over there, thought Rod--just over there--a hundred miles or so, is Minnetaki and the Post! Happy visions filled his mind all that afternoon as they traveled across the foot of the lake. Three weeks more and he would see his mother--and home. And Wabi was going with him! He seemed tireless; his spirits were never exhausted; he laughed, whistled, even attempted to sing. He wondered if Minnetaki would be very glad to see him. He knew that she would be glad--but how glad?

Two days more were spent in circling the lower end of the lake. Then their trail turned northward, and on the second evening after this, as the cold red sun was sinking in all that heatless glory of the great North's day-end, they came out upon a forest-clad ridge and looked down upon the House of Wabinosh.

And as they looked--and as the burning disk of the sun, falling down and down behind forest, mountain and plain, bade its last adieu to the land of the wild, there came to them, strangely clear and beautiful, the notes of a bugle.

And Wabi, listening, grew rigid with wonder. As the last notes died away the cheers that had been close to his lips gave way to the question, "What does that mean?"

"A bugle!" said Rod.

As he spoke there came to their ears the heavy, reverberating boom of a big gun.

"If I'm not mistaken," he added, "that is a sunset salute. I didn't know you had--soldiers--at the Post!"

"We haven't," replied the Indian youth. "By George, what do you suppose it means?"

He hurried down the ridge, the others close behind him. Fifteen minutes later they trailed out into the open near the Post. A strange change had occurred since Rod and his companions had last seen Wabinosh House. In the open half a dozen rude log shelters had been erected, and about these were scores of soldiers in the uniform of his Majesty, the King of England. Shouts of greeting died on the hunters' lips. They hastened to the dwelling of the factor, and while Wabi rushed in to meet his mother and father Rod cut across to the Company's store. He had often found Minnetaki there. But his present hope was shattered, and after looking in he turned back to the house. By the time he had reached the steps a second time the princess mother, with Wabi close behind her, came out to welcome him.

Wabi's face was flushed with excitement. His eyes sparkled.

"Rod, what do you think!" he exclaimed, after his mother had gone back to see to the preparation of their supper. "The government has declared war on the Woongas and has sent up a company of regulars to wipe 'em out! They have been murdering and robbing as never before during the last two months. The regulars start after them to-morrow!"

He was breathing hard and excitedly.

"Can't you stay--and join in the campaign?" he pleaded.

"I can't," replied Rod. "I can't, Wabi; I've got to go home. You know that. And you're going with me. The regulars can get along without you. Go back to Detroit with me--and get your mother to let Minnetaki go with us."

"Not now, Rod," said the Indian youth, taking his friend's hand. "I won't be able to go--now. Nor Minnetaki either. They have been having such desperate times here that father has sent her away. He wanted mother to go, but she wouldn't."

"Sent Minnetaki away?" gasped Rod.

"Yes. She started for Kenogami House four days ago in company with an Indian woman and three guides. That was undoubtedly their trail you found."

"And the footprint--"

"Was hers," laughed Wabi, putting an arm affectionately around his chum's shoulders. "Won't you stay, Rod?"

"It is impossible."

He went to his old room, and until suppertime sat alone in silent dejection. Two great disappointments had fallen upon him. Wabi could not go home with him--and he had missed Minnetaki. The young girl had left a note in her mother's care for him, and he read it again and again. She had written it believing that she would return to Wabinosh House before the hunters, but at the end she had added a paragraph in which she said that if she did not do this Rod must make the Post a second visit very soon, and bring his mother with him.

At supper the princess mother several times pressed Minnetaki's invitation upon the young hunter. She read to him parts of certain letters which she had received from Mrs. Drew during the winter, and Rod was overjoyed to find that his mother was not only in good health, but that she had given her promise to visit Wabinosh House the following summer. Wabi broke all table etiquette by giving vent to a warlike whoop of joy at this announcement, and once more Rod's spirits rose high above his temporary disappointments.

That night the furs were appraised and purchased by the factor for his Company, and Rod's share, including his third of the gold, was nearly seven hundred dollars. The next morning the bi-monthly sled party, was leaving for civilization, and he prepared to go with it, after writing a long letter to Minnetaki, which was to be carried to her by the faithful Mukoki. Most of that night Wabi and his friend sat up and talked, and made plans. It was believed that the campaign against the Woongas would be a short and decisive one. By spring all trouble would be over.

"And you'll come back as soon as you can?" pleaded Wabi for the hundredth time. "You'll come back by the time the ice breaks up?"

"If I am alive!" pledged the city youth.

"And you'll bring your mother?"

"She has promised."

"And then--for the gold!"

"For the gold!"

Wabi held out his hand and the two gripped heartily.

"And Minnetaki will be here then--I swear it!" said the Indian youth, laughing.

Rod blushed.

And that night alone he slipped quietly out into the still, white night; and he looked, longingly, far into the southeast where he had found the footprint in the snow; and he turned to the north, and the east, and the west, and lastly to the south, and his eyes seemed to travel through the distance of a thousand miles to where a home and a mother lay sleeping in a great city. And as he turned back to the House of Wabinosh, where all the lights were out, he spoke softly to himself:

"It's home--to-morrow!"

And then he added:

"But you bet I'll be back by the time the ice breaks up!"

www.bookjungle.com *email:* sales@bookjungle.com *fax:* 630-214-0564 *mail:* Book Jungle PO Box 2226 Champaign, IL 61825

The Codes Of Hammurabi And Moses
W. W. Davies

QTY

The discovery of the Hammurabi Code is one of the greatest achievements of archaeology, and is of paramount interest, not only to the student of the Bible, but also to all those interested in ancient history...

Religion　　**ISBN:** *1-59462-338-4*　　**Pages:** 132
　　　　　　　　　　　　　　　　　　　　　MSRP $12.95

The Theory of Moral Sentiments
Adam Smith

QTY

This work from 1749. contains original theories of conscience amd moral judgment and it is the foundation for systemof morals.

Philosophy　**ISBN:** *1-59462-777-0*　　**Pages:** 536
　　　　　　　　　　　　　　　　　　　　　MSRP $19.95

Jessica's First Prayer
Hesba Stretton

QTY

In a screened and secluded corner of one of the many railway-bridges which span the streets of London there could be seen a few years ago, from five o'clock every morning until half past eight, a tidily set-out coffee-stall, consisting of a trestle and board, upon which stood two large tin cans, with a small fire of charcoal burning under each so as to keep the coffee boiling during the early hours of the morning when the work-people were thronging into the city on their way to their daily toil...

Childrens　**ISBN:** *1-59462-373-2*　　**Pages:** 84
　　　　　　　　　　　　　　　　　　　　　MSRP $9.95

My Life and Work
Henry Ford

QTY

Henry Ford revolutionized the world with his implementation of mass production for the Model T automobile. Gain valuable business insight into his life and work with his own auto-biography... "We have only started on our development of our country we have not as yet, with all our talk of wonderful progress, done more than scratch the surface. The progress has been wonderful enough but..."

Biographies/　**ISBN:** *1-59462-198-5*　　**Pages:** 300
　　　　　　　　　　　　　　　　　　　　　MSRP $21.95

www.bookjungle.com email: sales@bookjungle.com fax: 630-214-0564 mail: Book Jungle PO Box 2226 Champaign, IL 61825

The Art of Cross-Examination
Francis Wellman

QTY

I presume it is the experience of every author, after his first book is published upon an important subject, to be almost overwhelmed with a wealth of ideas and illustrations which could readily have been included in his book, and which to his own mind, at least, seem to make a second edition inevitable. Such certainly was the case with me; and when the first edition had reached its sixth impression in five months, I rejoiced to learn that it seemed to my publishers that the book had met with a sufficiently favorable reception to justify a second and considerably enlarged edition. ..

Reference   ISBN: *1-59462-647-2*   Pages:412   MSRP $19.95

On the Duty of Civil Disobedience
Henry David Thoreau

QTY

Thoreau wrote his famous essay, On the Duty of Civil Disobedience, as a protest against an unjust but popular war and the immoral but popular institution of slave-owning. He did more than write—he declined to pay his taxes, and was hauled off to gaol in consequence. Who can say how much this refusal of his hastened the end of the war and of slavery ?

Law   ISBN: *1-59462-747-9*   Pages:48   MSRP $7.45

Dream Psychology Psychoanalysis for Beginners
Sigmund Freud

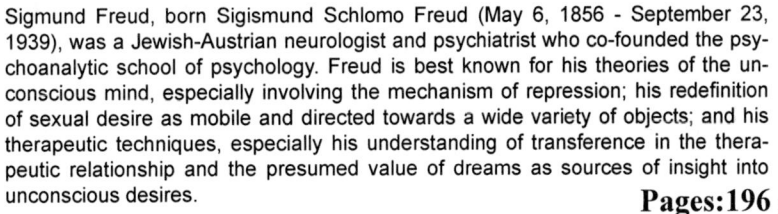

QTY

Sigmund Freud, born Sigismund Schlomo Freud (May 6, 1856 - September 23, 1939), was a Jewish-Austrian neurologist and psychiatrist who co-founded the psychoanalytic school of psychology. Freud is best known for his theories of the unconscious mind, especially involving the mechanism of repression; his redefinition of sexual desire as mobile and directed towards a wide variety of objects; and his therapeutic techniques, especially his understanding of transference in the therapeutic relationship and the presumed value of dreams as sources of insight into unconscious desires.

Psychology   ISBN: *1-59462-905-6*   Pages:196   MSRP $15.45

The Miracle of Right Thought
Orison Swett Marden

QTY

Believe with all of your heart that you will do what you were made to do. When the mind has once formed the habit of holding cheerful, happy, prosperous pictures, it will not be easy to form the opposite habit. It does not matter how improbable or how far away this realization may see, or how dark the prospects may be, if we visualize them as best we can, as vividly as possible, hold tenaciously to them and vigorously struggle to attain them, they will gradually become actualized, realized in the life. But a desire, a longing without endeavor, a yearning abandoned or held indifferently will vanish without realization.

Self Help   ISBN: *1-59462-644-8*   Pages:360   MSRP $25.45

www.bookjungle.com email: sales@bookjungle.com fax: 630-214-0564 mail: Book Jungle PO Box 2226 Champaign, IL 61825

QTY

	Title	ISBN	Price
☐	**The Rosicrucian Cosmo-Conception Mystic Christianity** by *Max Heindel*	ISBN: 1-59462-188-8	$38.95

The Rosicrucian Cosmo-conception is not dogmatic, neither does it appeal to any other authority than the reason of the student. It is: not controversial, but is: sent forth in the, hope that it may help to clear...
New Age/Religion Pages 646

| ☐ | **Abandonment To Divine Providence** by *Jean-Pierre de Caussade* | ISBN: 1-59462-228-0 | $25.95 |

"The Rev. Jean Pierre de Caussade was one of the most remarkable spiritual writers of the Society of Jesus in France in the 18th Century. His death took place at Toulouse in 1751. His works have gone through many editions and have been republished...
Inspirational/Religion Pages 400

| ☐ | **Mental Chemistry** by *Charles Haanel* | ISBN: 1-59462-192-6 | $23.95 |

Mental Chemistry allows the change of material conditions by combining and appropriately utilizing the power of the mind. Much like applied chemistry creates something new and unique out of careful combinations of chemicals the mastery of mental chemistry...
New Age Pages 354

| ☐ | **The Letters of Robert Browning and Elizabeth Barret Barrett 1845-1846 vol II** by *Robert Browning and Elizabeth Barrett* | ISBN: 1-59462-193-4 | $35.95 |

Biographies Pages 596

| ☐ | **Gleanings In Genesis (volume I)** by *Arthur W. Pink* | ISBN: 1-59462-130-6 | $27.45 |

Appropriately has Genesis been termed "the seed plot of the Bible" for in it we have, in germ form, almost all of the great doctrines which are afterwards fully developed in the books of Scripture which follow...
Religion/Inspirational Pages 420

| ☐ | **The Master Key** by *L. W. de Laurence* | ISBN: 1-59462-001-6 | $30.95 |

In no branch of human knowledge has there been a more lively increase of the spirit of research during the past few years than in the study of Psychology, Concentration and Mental Discipline. The requests for authentic lessons in Thought Control, Mental Discipline and...
New Age/Business Pages 422

| ☐ | **The Lesser Key Of Solomon Goetia** by *L. W. de Laurence* | ISBN: 1-59462-092-X | $9.95 |

This translation of the first book of the "Lernegton" which is here for the first time made accessible to students of Talismanic Magic was done, after careful collation and edition, from numerous Ancient Manuscripts in Hebrew, Latin, and French...
New Age/Occult Pages 92

| ☐ | **Rubaiyat Of Omar Khayyam** by *Edward Fitzgerald* | ISBN: 1-59462-332-5 | $13.95 |

Edward Fitzgerald, whom the world has already learned, in spite of his own efforts to remain within the shadow of anonymity, to look upon as one of the rarest poets of the century, was born at Bredfield, in Suffolk, on the 31st of March, 1809. He was the third son of John Purcell...
Music Pages 172

| ☐ | **Ancient Law** by *Henry Maine* | ISBN: 1-59462-128-4 | $29.95 |

The chief object of the following pages is to indicate some of the earliest ideas of mankind, as they are reflected in Ancient Law, and to point out the relation of those ideas to modern thought.
Religion/History Pages 452

| ☐ | **Far-Away Stories** by *William J. Locke* | ISBN: 1-59462-129-2 | $19.45 |

"Good wine needs no bush, but a collection of mixed vintages does. And this book is just such a collection. Some of the stories I do not want to remain buried for ever in the museum files of dead magazine-numbers an author's not unpardonable vanity..."
Fiction Pages 272

| ☐ | **Life of David Crockett** by *David Crockett* | ISBN: 1-59462-250-7 | $27.45 |

"Colonel David Crockett was one of the most remarkable men of the times in which he lived. Born in humble life, but gifted with a strong will, an indomitable courage, and unremitting perseverance...
Biographies New Age Pages 424

| ☐ | **Lip-Reading** by *Edward Nitchie* | ISBN: 1-59462-206-X | $25.95 |

Edward B. Nitchie, founder of the New York School for the Hard of Hearing, now the Nitchie School of Lip-Reading, Inc, wrote "LIP-READING Principles and Practice". The development and perfecting of this meritorious work on lip-reading was an undertaking...
How-to Pages 400

| ☐ | **A Handbook of Suggestive Therapeutics, Applied Hypnotism, Psychic Science** by *Henry Munro* | ISBN: 1-59462-214-0 | $24.95 |

Health/New Age Health Self-help Pages 376

| ☐ | **A Doll's House: and Two Other Plays** by *Henrik Ibsen* | ISBN: 1-59462-112-8 | $19.95 |

Henrik Ibsen created this classic when in revolutionary 1848 Rome. Introducing some striking concepts in playwriting for the realist genre, this play has been studied the world over.
Fiction/Classics/Plays 308

| ☐ | **The Light of Asia** by *sir Edwin Arnold* | ISBN: 1-59462-204-3 | $13.95 |

In this poetic masterpiece, Edwin Arnold describes the life and teachings of Buddha. The man who was to become known as Buddha to the world was born as Prince Gautama of India but he rejected the worldly riches and abandoned the reigns of power when...
Religion/History/Biographies Pages 170

| ☐ | **The Complete Works of Guy de Maupassant** by *Guy de Maupassant* | ISBN: 1-59462-157-8 | $16.95 |

"For days and days, nights and nights, I had dreamed of that first kiss which was to consecrate our engagement, and I knew not on what spot I should put my lips..."
Fiction/Classics Pages 240

| ☐ | **The Art of Cross-Examination** by *Francis L. Wellman* | ISBN: 1-59462-309-0 | $26.95 |

Written by a renowned trial lawyer, Wellman imparts his experience and uses case studies to explain how to use psychology to extract desired information through questioning.
How-to/Science Reference Pages 408

| ☐ | **Answered or Unanswered?** by *Louisa Vaughan* | ISBN: 1-59462-248-5 | $10.95 |

Miracles of Faith in China
Religion Pages 112

| ☐ | **The Edinburgh Lectures on Mental Science (1909)** by *Thomas* | ISBN: 1-59462-008-3 | $11.95 |

This book contains the substance of a course of lectures recently given by the writer in the Queen Street Hall, Edinburgh. Its purpose is to indicate the Natural Principles governing the relation between Mental Action and Material Conditions...
New Age/Psychology Pages 148

| ☐ | **Ayesha** by *H. Rider Haggard* | ISBN: 1-59462-301-5 | $24.95 |

Verily and indeed it is the unexpected that happens! Probably if there was one person upon the earth from whom the Editor of this, and of a certain previous history, did not expect to hear again...
Classics Pages 380

| ☐ | **Ayala's Angel** by *Anthony Trollope* | ISBN: 1-59462-352-X | $29.95 |

The two girls were both pretty, but Lucy who was twenty-one who supposed to be simple and comparatively unattractive, whereas Ayala was credited, as her Bombwhat romantic name might show, with poetic charm and a taste for romance. Ayala when her father died was nineteen...
Fiction Pages 484

| ☐ | **The American Commonwealth** by *James Bryce* | ISBN: 1-59462-286-8 | $34.45 |

An interpretation of American democratic political theory. It examines political mechanics and society from the perspective of Scotsman James Bryce
Politics Pages 572

| ☐ | **Stories of the Pilgrims** by *Margaret P. Pumphrey* | ISBN: 1-59462-116-0 | $17.95 |

This book explores pilgrims religious oppression in England as well as their escape to Holland and eventual crossing to America on the Mayflower, and their early days in New England...
History Pages 268

www.bookjungle.com email: sales@bookjungle.com fax: 630-214-0564 mail: Book Jungle PO Box 2226 Champaign, IL 61825

QTY

The Fasting Cure *by Sinclair Upton*   ISBN: *1-59462-222-1* $13.95
In the Cosmopolitan Magazine for May, 1910, and in the Contemporary Review (London) for April, 1910, I published an article dealing with my experiences in fasting. I have written a great many magazine articles, but never one which attracted so much attention... *New Age/Self Help/Health Pages 164*

Hebrew Astrology *by Sepharial*   ISBN: *1-59462-308-2* $13.45
In these days of advanced thinking it is a matter of common observation that we have left many of the old landmarks behind and that we are now pressing forward to greater heights and to a wider horizon than that which represented the mind-content of our progenitors... *Astrology Pages 144*

Thought Vibration or The Law of Attraction in the Thought World   ISBN: *1-59462-127-6* $12.95
by William Walker Atkinson   *Psychology/Religion Pages 144*

Optimism *by Helen Keller*   ISBN: *1-59462-108-X* $15.95
Helen Keller was blind, deaf, and mute since 19 months old, yet famously learned how to overcome these handicaps, communicate with the world, and spread her lectures promoting optimism. An inspiring read for everyone... *Biographies/Inspirational Pages 84*

Sara Crewe *by Frances Burnett*   ISBN: *1-59462-360-0* $9.45
In the first place, Miss Minchin lived in London. Her home was a large, dull, tall one, in a large, dull square, where all the houses were alike, and all the sparrows were alike, and where all the door-knockers made the same heavy sound... *Childrens/Classic Pages 88*

The Autobiography of Benjamin Franklin *by Benjamin Franklin*   ISBN: *1-59462-135-7* $24.95
The Autobiography of Benjamin Franklin has probably been more extensively read than any other American historical work, and no other book of its kind has had such ups and downs of fortune. Franklin lived for many years in England, where he was agent... *Biographies/History Pages 332*

Name	
Email	
Telephone	
Address	
City, State ZIP	

☐ Credit Card   ☐ Check / Money Order

Credit Card Number	
Expiration Date	
Signature	

Please Mail to: Book Jungle
                  PO Box 2226
                  Champaign, IL 61825
or Fax to: 630-214-0564

ORDERING INFORMATION
web: *www.bookjungle.com*
email: *sales@bookjungle.com*
fax: *630-214-0564*
mail: *Book Jungle PO Box 2226 Champaign, IL 61825*
or PayPal *to sales@bookjungle.com*

Please contact us for bulk discounts

DIRECT-ORDER TERMS

**20% Discount if You Order
Two or More Books**
Free Domestic Shipping!
Accepted: Master Card, Visa,
Discover, American Express

CPSIA information can be obtained at www.ICGtesting.com
Printed in the USA
LVOW071917010712
288415LV00003B/41/P

9 781438 518060